The Redesigned Ranch

 Horseshoe Home Ranch

LIZ ISAACSON

ISBN-13: 978-1-63876-238-6

"Heal me, O Lord, and I shall be healed; save me, and I shall be saved: for thou art my praise."

— JEREMIAH 17:14

CHAPTER 1

*T*he chilled bite of the winter wind pulled against Jace Lovell's cowboy hat, causing him to reach up and press one palm firmly on top of his head to keep it in place. A native of Gold Valley, Montana—and now the foreman at Horseshoe Home Ranch that spread partway up one of the mountains that surrounded the valley—Jace understood the weather. Almost like he and Mother Nature had come to an agreement.

But he didn't smile at the drifts of snow along the path leading from his cabin to the administration lodge or the promise of more wet weather. He wasn't planning on smiling at all. Because today, he had to conduct interviews to hire an interior designer to "renovate everything."

Yep, those were the directions he'd received from the ranch owner's wife, Gloria Brush. *Renovate everything.* Cowboy cabins—including his—the administration lodge, even the organization and flow of the tack rooms, and stables, and barns. *Everything.*

And Jace, as foreman, had to sit through an entire day of interviews. Caged between the walls, when he could be feeding cattle, or sweeping out horse stalls, or almost anything but talking to people and sitting in a chair all day.

At least the interior designers were coming to him. He climbed the stairs to the administration lodge—which functioned and looked just fine to him—and pushed through the door. A rush of heated air warmed his skin, driving away the icy chill that had kissed his cheeks. He lifted his hat, ran his fingers through his dark hair, and settled the hat back into place.

The lodge buzzed with activity. In anticipation of the upcoming interviews, he had the boys organizing tables and chairs this morning. He took a deep breath and tried to imagine the spacious building differently. But he didn't have the eye or mind of a designer and couldn't really picture anything that wasn't already there. Surely the designer wouldn't be satisfied with functionality, oh, no. Leave it to Gloria to try to make a cattle ranch feel like a day spa.

Jace wasn't entirely sure why Gloria wanted to remodel, and a skin of worry encased him. Were they preparing to sell Horseshoe Home? What would become of him if they did? He'd just gotten his footing as foreman and he'd grown up on the ranch as his father had been foreman before Jace.

He squared his shoulders and dismissed his rampant worries. He'd ask Gloria why she wanted the renovation the next chance he got. No sense in worrying about it until then.

As he glanced around, he noticed that the carpet was worn, but this was a working ranch with two-dozen cowboys coming and going. The walls had been repainted a bright white just last year. He'd spearheaded that campaign during one of the worst weather weeks Montana had ever witnessed. Besides feeding and watering the livestock, the cowboys stayed indoors. Sixty degrees below zero would do that to a ranch.

The high ceilings bore the skeleton of the majestic wooden structure, with exposed beams slanting toward the pinnacle of the roof. Desks and chairs littered the open space out front, and doorways lined the perimeter. See, the lodge used to be the homestead. So the kitchen had stayed put, but the large dining room had been set up as a break room of sorts, where cowboys could eat lunch or relax.

The bedrooms down the hall functioned as offices for the accountant, the foreman, and the owner. The open living area had become their meeting room, and a few of the cowboys had desks to keep sales reports, folders of information about feed supplies, and whatever else they needed to do their particular job well.

"All set, boss." Landon, the tall former rodeo star approached Jace. "I even had Howie clean the bathrooms."

The owner had a cleaning service come through the lodge every week, but they weren't scheduled to come until Thursday—and that was nowhere near enough with thirty men using the building day in and day out.

"Thanks." Jace made his voice as friendly as he could, because he couldn't get his lips to curve upward. "And we'll be meeting them—" He glanced toward the flurry of activity in the open area to his left. "In my office?"

"You said you didn't care where, and there's a storm blowin' in...." Landon cut a look toward a couple of rowdier cowhands, but they didn't notice. "We'll have the feeding done in an hour and then Rob said we could put on a movie after that while it snows."

Jace fisted his hand so he wouldn't pinch the bridge of his nose. It was only Monday—he had a long week ahead of him, if showing movies was any indication.

"Thought the best place for that was here," Landon said. "But I can—"

"It's fine, Landon." Jace had asked him to get things set up and keep the cowboys busy. "I guess I'll be in my office. Will you show the first applicant back when they arrive?"

"Sure thing, boss," Landon called after him, as Jace had already started walking away. He maneuvered through the maze and escaped down the hall. His office sat through the first door on the right, and a sense of calm prevailed after he shut the door. He closed his eyes and thought, *Help me get through this day.*

He wasn't terribly religious, but since his brother, Tom, had moved back to Gold Valley, Jace had been attending church with him and his family. Maybe some of the pastor's words about prayer had infused into Jace's mind.

No matter what, he felt calmer as he settled behind his desk, ran his hands down his face and over his beard, and opened the first folder. He'd prepared them on Saturday afternoon after he'd de-iced the outdoor watering troughs. He hadn't had a chance to review every applicant, and he probably wouldn't be able to finish that job before the first applicant arrived for her interview.

Jace had known enough to ask for a portfolio from each applicant, and he flipped the page to see what this first one had designed. So many pastels met his eye he wondered if he'd been swallowed by a rainbow. He could not imagine walking into a cowboy cabin only to be greeted by sea green walls and lavender cabinets.

Wild hope that the approaching storm would keep the applicants in town tore through him. Maybe he could put this off until another day. He closed the folder just as someone knocked on the door. Heart sinking, he called, "C'mon in."

The door opened, showing Landon standing just to the side of the doorway. "Right in there, ma'am."

A woman entered, her dark hair plaited, with the end of her braid riding over her shoulder. She wore a professional pantsuit and carried a leather briefcase purse. Sourness stained the back of Jace's throat. She wasn't Wendy, but her clothing and accessory selections reminded him so much of his ex that Jace thought seriously about bolting.

After all, that was what she'd done.

He stuffed his emotions down to the bottom of his steel-tipped cowboy boots and stood. "Hello." He tried not to feel intimidated by her, but the truth was, the feeling that he was outclassed in every sense of the word flowed through him like a fast-moving river.

His panic only increased as the interview commenced. He made it through, told Miss Purple Pastel that he'd let her know very soon, and let her go. He pulled the door closed behind her, and Jace paced back to the window. Sure enough, fat flakes had started to drift down to the ground, adding to the already high piles of snow.

His thoughts fled to Wendy, as they always did when he let his guard down. She'd left him after three years together. Left him standing at the altar by himself—oh, and half the town in attendance. Left him for a more exciting life and career in Los Angeles. Everything about that designer reminded him of Wendy, and for that reason alone—not to mention the horrendous pastels—he couldn't hire her.

Another knock sounded. Another woman entered. Another interview started. Miss Wood Nymph favored dark woods and light, gauzy materials. Jace wondered if such curtains would withstand a single day against twenty-four cowhands.

Miss Giddy bubbled into the room with giggles and grins, spoke the same way, and left in a cloud of expensive-smelling perfume. By lunch, Jace knew today was shaping up to be the worst day he'd ever experienced on the ranch. And he hated that, because the ranch was his safe haven. The one place Wendy hadn't permeated, hadn't poisoned, hadn't permanently altered in his life.

Three more interviews, and still Jace didn't see something in the folders—or the applicants—he thought might fit at Horseshoe Home. Finally, only one folder remained on his desk. He didn't bother to open it. All the designers had brought a copy of their designs for the different spaces on the ranch.

Landon opened the door and said, "Miss Belle."

Jace snapped his head up, ice sinking through his chest, coating his lungs and internal organs in stiff blocks he'd never escape. Why hadn't—?

"Well, look at *you*." Belle strode forward, her luxurious auburn hair flowing behind her like a curtain. She'd pinned back only the very front, leaving the rest to frame her high cheekbones, her bright green eyes, and her very glossed lips.

Jace yanked his attention away from those lips, which had always intrigued him. "Look at me?" he asked, making a conscious effort not to reach up and smooth down his beard like he did when he wanted to look his best. "Look at you. What happened? Did Sacramento run out of red lipstick? You had to come all the way to Gold Valley to get stocked up?"

"Ha ha." She swept him from head to toe. "I see you're still wearing that ridiculous hat."

"Everyone wears these hats," he shot back. "We're cowboys."

"Yes, well, most *decent* men buy a replacement every few years." She sniffed as she perched on the edge of the chair across from his desk and pulled a folder from her purse. No briefcase bag. No pretentious heels—Belle didn't need them. She stood almost as tall as her brother, Landon.

The snake, Jace thought as he rounded the desk and took

his seat. Landon should've told him his sister had applied. Growing up, Jace had never seen eye-to-eye with the redhead, though he did enjoy trading jabs with her when she visited from her hoity-toity job at a design firm in Sacramento.

Instead of focusing on her tight black jeans and flowing top of cobalt blue—which he thought made her hair look positively decadent—he flipped open the folder to check her address. "You moved back?"

She shrugged one shoulder, the silky blouse she wore slipping a little. "My parents are on a six-month service mission in Africa. I'm taking care of the house."

He returned his gaze to the folder, which was safer than drinking in Belle's curves. "Mm hm." He'd heard that before. Pretty princess left home, and instead of admitting that the world had chewed her up, she came home "to take care of the house."

"You must be tired." Her tone, which someone less experienced than Jace could've misinterpreted to be sympathetic, caused him to abandon the folder.

"Why do you say that?" Jace knew Belle's body didn't actually house sympathetic bones, even though she dressed it up nice and sprayed intoxicating, lilac-scented perfume across her collarbone. His gaze dropped to that spot, and her golden skin made his blood run a little faster.

"You didn't even make a joke about me taking care of the house."

Jace opened his mouth to say something, but closed it when nothing came to mind. "It's been a long day. Let's get this over with." With effort, he closed her folder and shoved his traitorous thoughts about Belle's attractiveness to the back of his mind. "Did you bring your portfolio?"

————

Belle's stomach flipped and flopped like a fish someone had left to die on the shore. Jace took forever to look at her portfolio, and he knew it. Was enjoying making her wait on him—just like he always had. At least not everything in Belle's world had exploded when she'd lost her job in Sacramento. It only felt that way, especially being back in her hometown and having to see everyone who'd never left.

"What's the last thing you worked on?" he asked, the slow rumble of his voice sending a shiver through her body.

Belle smiled, and it actually felt real on her face. "I did an old ranch-style house near the Redwoods. Beautiful setting. Trees everywhere. Lots of natural wood." She slid an oversized sheet toward him. The vibrant photos didn't do the place justice. She'd loved that property, the serenity she'd felt in those woods. In truth, she'd been hoping to recapture some of those feelings in Gold Valley, which boasted of the same slow pace of life, similar mountains and trees and peace.

"This is nice, Belle." He glanced up at her. Not long enough to truly make eye contact, but she heard the sincerity in his voice. She basked in the compliment, as she hadn't had many in a long time.

"Nice?" came out of her mouth. She cursed her quick wit

—and Jace Lovell. He seemed to bring out the sharpest edge to her tongue.

His eyes came up more slowly this time and sank into hers. She could lose herself in the deep, dark depths of them —if she were anywhere close to even thinking about dating a man. And even if she was, he would most certainly not be a rancher, a friend of her brother's, or Jace Lovell. Three strikes against him.

He's out, she told herself firmly.

Still, he had beautiful eyes. And a full beard she wanted to trace her fingers through. "It's more than nice. That's gorgeous work."

"Gorgeous?" He turned the paper over as if there'd be evidence of gorgeousness on the back. "I guess you're the expert." He put it unceremoniously in the folder and closed the file. "I'll let you know soon."

"How many applicants did you have?" She leaned back and crossed her legs. Just because he was the interviewer didn't mean she couldn't ask some of her own questions.

He stared at her, and she didn't entirely hate the way his gaze seemed to see past all of her carefully crafted defenses. "'Bout eight, I reckon."

"You reckon?" She laughed. "It's a number," she said. "It's either seven, or eight, or nine. There's no guessing at it."

He came around the desk and sat on the edge of it, his powerful presence combined with the delicious scent of his cologne nearly knocking Belle backward. She straightened her spine to maintain her position, especially when he crossed those enormous arms. He must eat a pound of meat for every meal to keep muscles like that.

"Since we're keeping track of torture," he growled. "Eight."

"Are any of them better than me?"

"All of 'em."

Her heart sank, though she knew Jace had only said that to rub at her. Maybe he had seen her extreme insecurity when he stared at her. She swallowed hard, trying to find her center and pull all her masks back in place.

Finally, she stood and tossed her purse strap over her shoulder. "Well, it's been a pleasure, Mister Lovell." She made her voice sticky sweet and as Southern as possible. She flounced toward the door, turning back with her hand on the knob. "You still oiling your beard?"

She didn't wait for him to answer. She flung him a smirk and practically ran from his office before he could respond. Ooh, that'd make him mad. A tug of regret pulled through her, but she couldn't afford for him to see anything but the powerhouse Belle had been when she'd gone off to Sacramento to conquer the world.

Belle noticed the traveling eyes of the cowboys who watched her as she wove through the desks, tables, and chairs toward the exit. Landon had kept them all at bay since she'd returned to Gold Valley two weeks ago.

Isn't that just like Jace not to know I'd come home? she thought as she faced the winter storm. Indignation filled her, marred by a tiny part of her that simply felt wounded. Sure, she and Jace weren't going to text and hang out, but she considered him a friend. Maybe not a close one, or one she actually wanted to spend much time with, but at least someone who should've known she'd come back.

As she drove along the sloppy ruts in the road toward civilization, she remembered that she hadn't seen him at all either. Not at church, though she'd only gone once and sat in the balcony so she could escape quicker. Not in town. Nowhere. Landon had told her he was the foreman now, so maybe that kept him busier than she would have thought.

Please help me get this job. Her fingers turned white from her death grip on the steering wheel, and a rush of fear made her wish she could recall her poisoned words about Jace's beard. Even if he did oil it, she shouldn't have said so —not if she wanted to get the job. She turned back onto the paved, snow-plowed highway and headed for the town of Gold Valley, her mind churning.

Maybe she should go back. Apologize about the beard comment. Her mouth turned dry at the thought of maybe tracing her fingertips along Jace's jaw…. Her phone chimed as she made it out of the canyon. Six texts from her new supervisor at the design firm had come in at the same time. She realized she didn't have cell service in the canyon or up at the ranch, and hurried to call him back.

"Hey, Calvin," she said when he answered.

"Where have you been? The samples for the Montgomery cabin came in, and I need you here."

"You sent me out to Horseshoe Home Ranch." The saucy side of Belle almost added, "Remember?" but she managed to swallow the word back before it came out. She would've said it to Jace, but Calvin was as far from Jace as someone could get. He wouldn't appreciate it—but he didn't have the authority to cut her loose because of it.

"Oh, right." Shuffling came through the line, and Belle suspected his attention had already shifted to something else. "How did it go?"

"Great," Belle said, hoping she wasn't fibbing. "He said I'd know soon."

"I hope so," Calvin said. "You need to book a client."

I know, she wanted to scream. Calvin had made his opinion of her very clear, and he wasn't impressed. She came with no loyal clients, no prospects, no accounts, and hardly any experience. A year in the Sacramento firm, where she'd basically been an intern to the top designer there, hadn't exactly catapulted her career.

"I feel good about it." Her voice sounded false and too bright to her own ears.

"Feeling good about something doesn't mean much."

"I'll be back to the office in a few minutes." One glance at the clock on her dashboard told her she should've finished work fifteen minutes ago. But when Calvin called....

"No need," he said. "We'll go over these samples first thing in the morning. Don't forget my coffee." He hung up before Belle could confirm.

Steam practically leaked from her ears. She was his colleague, not his secretary. She paid for her own desk space, same as he did. He brought in more money to the conglomerate, sure. But that didn't mean she had to bring him coffee. In fact, he'd "asked" her several times to bring him a cappuccino, and each time she'd "forgotten."

She'd "forget" tomorrow too, even though her forgetfulness probably lowered his opinion of her. "Can't get much lower," she muttered to herself as she rounded the corner and came face-to-face with the horseshoe-shaped waterfalls. Past them, she finally saw the outskirts of town ahead.

Belle didn't care. She wasn't going to take the guy coffee. She'd land the account at Horseshoe Home, and start saving to open her own design company. She knew she was a good designer—better than anyone else in Gold Valley. She'd signed on with the design firm for legitimacy, to have a name to put on her business cards, but she dreamed of having her name speak for itself, her own name on her stationery, on the side of a building.

She prayed again for help from the Lord as the desperation to accomplish all she hoped to do crowded her lungs and made her gasp for air.

CHAPTER 2

The next morning, Belle arrived before Calvin, as usual. Didn't matter. The owner of Crescent Moon, the one and only design firm in Gold Valley, didn't show up until after noon. So the owner never knew who arrived first to work—though in the past two weeks, Belle had beaten everybody through the front door.

Calvin walked in just after nine, saw her at her desk, and frowned. Like he usually did.

"Morning, Calvin," she chirped from behind her laptop. "I waited to go through the samples with you. Meanwhile, I found a hotel on the east side of town that's looking for a remodel. I'm just finishing my proposal for them."

He harrumphed, noticed the lack of coffee, and his frown lines deepened. "Did you forget something this morning?"

Belle made a show of checking her desk, even tipping her laptop down as she attempted to look as confused as possible. "I don't think so...." She reached for her travel mug of decaf and took a sip. "Did you?"

A silent battle of wills ensued, which ended when Calvin sighed and headed for the largest storage room, where the samples waited. Satisfied and victorious, Belle got up to follow him. They spoke about the Montgomery cabin, the design desired by the owner, and the practicality of some of the items they'd ordered.

Belle fingered the edge of a high-end curtain, her mind wandering to what her own home would look like one day. In Sacramento, she'd been building her dream home—well, apartment—one small room at a time. She'd had the entryway perfect, with an engineered hardwood in a dark oak color, a custom runner from the best rug-maker out of Phoenix, and an antique buffet that functioned as a side table for her décor, keys, and unopened mail.

She'd brought what she could from her apartment, but the perfect view and ideal layout couldn't be replicated in her childhood home despite it being five times larger. The very thought of going back to that house, alone, tonight made Belle consider sleeping at the office.

The youngest of three children, Belle had moved to Cal-State immediately upon graduation and got a jump-start on her interior design degree. She hadn't been at the top of her class, but was good enough to land a position at the prestigious design firm of Spencer Stallings.

She sighed, which earned her a glance from Calvin. "Everything okay with that granite?"

"I think it's too dark," she said, forcing herself to focus

on the here-and-now instead of the what-could've-been-if-she-hadn't-been-wronged. She'd made peace with it. Almost.

"It's almost metallic," she added. "I think Rayanne would like something with more gray shades, maybe a marbled effect." She'd met with the client, had taken copious notes about her likes and dislikes, her vision for the cabin. But Belle's real intuition came simply from talking with a person, looking at what they already had hanging on their walls, and asking them about their life. No, Rayanne definitely wouldn't like the glittering, dark granite.

"Well, see what George has."

Belle nodded and they moved on to backsplash tiles for the kitchens, the bathrooms, the indoor hot tub. Working on one cabin in the exclusive community on the mountainside certainly wasn't going to help Belle's fantasies of someday being able to afford a place like that, a place she could decorate however she wanted.

The work day ended without a call from Jace. Belle tasted bitterness on the back of her tongue. Landon had told her they needed to hire a designer quickly. Belle couldn't believe eight designers had put in for the job in the short timeframe. She'd only found out about it on Friday afternoon, rushed through her proposal so she could be on the interview list for yesterday. She supposed in Gold Valley, the independent designer had to constantly have her ear to the ground.

And now Jace hadn't called. How long would he take to make a decision?

She'd grown up with the Lovell boys, knew all about them. They'd both grown into quiet, strong men, who worked the ranch where their daddy raised them. As she turned into her parents' driveway and opened the garage, Belle wondered if Jace ever dreamed of doing something different, living somewhere else, starting over.

"Probably not," she told the empty house as she entered it. He was the type who did what he wanted, thought for himself. If he'd wanted to leave Gold Valley, he would have.

Her phone rang as she heated a frozen dinner for one in the microwave. She glanced at the screen and saw Jace's name. Her appetite vanished; her stomach swooped; her heart hammered.

"Hey, Jace," she said after swiping to connect the call.

"Belle."

She closed her eyes and conjured up his handsome face with that square jaw and straight nose. She could admit she'd thought about what his hair and beard would feel like between her fingers, against her lips. After all, Jace Lovell was a ten in the looks department.

"You gonna say anything?" she asked. "Or just breathe through the line all night?"

"You sure don't make things easy, do you?"

"Easy for who?"

"Look, if we're gonna work together, you can't argue with me about everything." His words punched the air right out of her lungs.

"Work together?" she managed to rasp. "Are you offering

me the job?" She hadn't dared to hope. She knew how dangerous and hard hope was to recover if lost.

"Against my better judgment, I am. You're the best designer who applied."

"Then why is hiring me against your better judgment?" She cocked her hip like he stood there and could see her.

"Because you make my blood boil just by lookin' at me."

"I can't help it if you have a funny face."

"See? It's that kind of smack-talk you can't do. I just want the renovation to go quickly and be easy. Can you do that or not?"

"Quick and easy?" Disbelief coated her words. "I don't think I've ever done anything quick and easy."

"Is that a threat?"

Belle exhaled. "You know you set my blood on fire too, right? Of course it's not a threat. I was just saying that if you're going to get the best cowboy cabins, the most beautiful lodge, and the most functional barns and stables, it won't happen quickly or easily. It takes a lot of work and a lot of time."

He sighed like someone had punctured his lungs with a sharp object and the air was slowly hissing out. "And you're gonna do all this work?"

"Absolutely."

A pause came through the line. It lasted so long, Belle thought she'd lost him. Even checked to make sure the call hadn't disconnected. It hadn't.

"You think you can work with me, Belle? I promise I'll be...nice."

Something softened inside Belle at the vulnerability she heard in his voice. "Jace, you're always nice."

"Am I?"

"It's just banter. I like you fine. And I can work with you, no problem." A horrible thought crossed her mind. "Can you work with me? I'd hate for you to have boiling blood all the time." She covered her own insecurity about being like-able with sarcasm, as she usually did.

"I'll be fine."

"Great. So will I."

"So it's a deal. I'll need you to come out to the ranch and sign some papers."

"What's the weather like tomorrow?"

"Supposed to storm all day."

Belle thought of her two-seater convertible she'd bought her second summer in California. "Maybe I'll wait—"

"So I'll see you tomorrow. Say, eleven o'clock?" He hung up before she could confirm or deny.

A knife of hot annoyance stabbed her right between her ribs. "That Jace Lovell," she muttered as she nearly slammed her phone down onto the ugly laminate countertop. She sensed a pattern of one-upmanship starting. She'd need to put a stop to that, and throwing him an insult as she walked out yesterday had been a very bad idea.

She'd make it up to him. A smile curved her lips as a plan formed in her mind. She was determined not to repeat the mistakes she'd made in Sacramento. She'd started by not letting Calvin treat her like a secretary. Now that she'd landed her first solo account, she wouldn't let anything or anyone get in her way of delivering exactly what the client wanted. And that started with sweetening up Jace a little.

———

Jace glanced toward his open office door when the scent of cinnamon met his nose. No one had authorized cooking in the kitchen today and the cowhands didn't generally season with cinnamon anyhow.

He went back to work—the third day in a row behind walls. He'd find out where the scent came from soon enough. He always did. As the foreman, nothing happened on the ranch without his eventual knowledge.

A few minutes later, a light knock sounded on his door and Belle stepped into his office. He'd been expecting her, but not for another fifteen minutes. The sight of her tall, curvy frame standing in his doorway rendered him breathless. He commanded himself to put on his usual mask, his protection the past six months since Wendy had left him looking the fool at his own wedding.

He noticed Belle's laughing eyes, the waves she'd added to her hair, the slim cut of her skirt and blouse. He startled again. When had he started looking at Belle like that? *Never*, he told himself. *You've never seen her like that.*

Mature and happy, she wore her success well. It made her beautiful and bright, like a new penny.

She beamed at him, and against his will, he smiled back. "Mornin'. You make it out here all right?"

"Obviously I did." She moved into his office and held a plate toward him. "I came armed with your favorite." She set the plate on his desk. "Oatmeal with dark chocolate chips."

He looked at the cookies like they might grow legs and attack. When they didn't, he glanced back at her. "How did you know?"

She fell into the chair opposite him. "I have my ways."

"You called Tom."

"Nope." She grinned. "Landon."

"Traitor," Jace said under his breath. "He told you about the job, too, right?"

"Yes." Her smile faded. "You said I was the best applicant. You're not mad he told me, are you?"

Jace couldn't say he was, because the truth was exactly the opposite. His heart pumped out an extra beat, and *that* angered him. "No," he said stiffly. He wasn't dating right now, maybe never again. He didn't want Belle to know about the fiasco with Wendy—she wasn't here when it happened and possibly hadn't heard yet.

Yet, his mind whispered. And in a town the size of Gold Valley, she'd find out. He might as well be the one to tell her. Still he sat silently drinking in the beautiful woman before him and trying to make sense of his jumbled emotions while controlling his raging hormones.

He'd never felt anything but frustration and fury with Belle Edmunds. How had that changed?

"So." He cleared his throat and nearly knocked the paperwork to the floor in his haste to grab it. "I need you to sign this. We have a budget of seven-hundred-fifty-thousand dollars, firm. We need the fourteen cabins redone, this building, and the three stables and attached barns." He slid the folder toward her, glad his fingers had something constructive to do. When he'd spoken with Gloria yesterday, she'd laughed when he'd asked if she was preparing to sell Horseshoe Home Ranch.

"Of course not." Her tinkling giggle still rang in Jace's ears. "It's been forty years since we've done anything to this place." She cocked her head at him. "We're just updating, Jace."

Just updating. His relief had been strong and overwhelming.

"Jace?"

He blinked at Belle. "I'm sorry, what?"

She blinked back at him. "Seven-hundred-fifty-thousand?"

He cleared his throat. "That's firm," he repeated. "Not a penny more. I'll be checking everything with the help of our accountant." When she continued gaping at him, he asked, "Is that enough?"

That snapped her into motion. She grabbed the pen. "It's plenty. Thanks." She flashed him a brilliant smile that punched holes in his plan to stay away from women. Desire *for Belle* poured through him, leaving him all together confused and slow-witted.

She flipped pages and signed her name where he'd marked the lines with little flags. "This says you're hiring Crescent Moon," she said, glancing up.

"That's right," he said, relieved that his voice stayed even. "You're the contact there, but we're basically hiring your firm. You know, to basically vouch for you in case you...." He waved his hand in a nonchalant gesture. "Mess up."

"I'm not going to mess up." Her jaw worked and her eyes blazed with green fire.

Jace leaned forward, hoping to avoid getting burned by the wrath he saw in her gaze. "I didn't say you will. It's a standard contract. That's why you work for a firm, isn't it?"

She deflated as quickly as she'd fired up. "Yes, of course." She signed her name for a final time and slapped the folder closed.

Jace took it and slid it in his desk drawer. "Great." He stood. "You want to stay for lunch? Landon said Miss Gloria is bringin' down a pot of chili for everyone."

Belle's grin nearly took his legs out from under him. "I've never met a chili I didn't like."

He chuckled and waited for her to exit the office before him. It was a gentlemanly gesture, he told himself. Definitely not so he could walk in her wake and breathe in the tantalizing scent of her perfume. Definitely not because of that.

Tom opened the door, nearly losing it to the wicked wind. "Come in, come in," he called.

Jace wasted no time stepping through the door. Tom wrestled it closed and set the locks. "You might be sleepin' here," he said. "That storm's turned nasty."

"You've finished the basement, right?" Jace shed his winter coat as Tom had a fire roaring in the hearth. "Something smells amazing."

"Rose made chocolate pie for dessert."

A pang of jealousy sliced through his stomach and chest with a speed Jace hadn't thought possible. "That's great."

"And yes, I finished the basement over Christmas," Tom said as he passed Jace and crossed the living room toward the kitchen. "Two bedrooms down there. You'll be comfortable if we go build a fire right now."

"I don't need to stay." Jace followed his brother. He'd wanted to stay at first. Loved spending time with Tom now that he'd returned to Montana. But suddenly the thought of existing in this happy-happy space made him anything but joyful. It only reminded him of everything he'd lost. Not all physical things either, but things like having someone to talk to, and someone to come home to, and the ability to believe in himself. He'd lost that. Lost his confidence, too. Lost a lot when Wendy left.

Rose turned from the stove. "Hey, Jace." Warmth radiated from her as Jace stepped into her embrace.

"Hey." He grinned at her. "Where's Mari?"

Rose exchanged a glance with Tom. "In her room." She

spooned stew into a bowl and handed it to Jace. "We'll eat without her tonight."

"I can—"

"Tom," Rose said. "She'll be fine. She made her choice."

Tom nodded, his mouth set in a tight line, and Jace felt like he was intruding. "I hired an interior designer today," he said. He hadn't planned on talking tonight. It was one of the things he loved best about eating dinner with Tom and Rose. No one pressured him to talk all the time, the way his mother did.

"Oh, yeah?" Tom sat at the dining room table with his bowl of stew. Rose placed a platter of cornbread on the table, a plate of butter, and a pitcher of punch. Jace had eaten cornbread with his chili for lunch, but in his opinion, one could never consume too much cornbread. He took two slices and slathered them with butter.

"Yeah," he said between bites. "Belle Edmunds. Remember her?"

Tom nearly choked. "Remember her?" He glanced at Rose, who still stood at the stove scooping up her own bowl of stew. "Every man within a hundred miles remembers Belle Edmunds."

Jace had difficulty swallowing. "Really? Why's that?"

"Maybe because she's drop-dead gorgeous," Tom whispered. "And smart. And—" Rose sat at the table, her gaze as sharp as Jace's father's had been when he'd caught the teenaged brothers sneaking off the ranch one summer night.

"Who are you boys talkin' about?"

"My new interior designer," Jace said, ignoring Tom's desperate look. "For the record, she's not that pretty." The lie coated his tongue and made the cornbread stick in his throat. He forced it down anyway.

"You think she's pretty?" Rose asked Tom.

"She is." He shrugged. "I mean, I haven't seen her since high school, but she was pretty then."

Jace wouldn't describe Belle with something as mundane as *pretty*. Tom had gotten it right with *drop-dead gorgeous*. "Even if she is pretty, she wouldn't be interested in me. *Especially* if she's pretty."

"Of course she would," Rose said. "Why wouldn't she be?"

Jace had a myriad of answers for that question, but he kept them all to himself. Tom and Rose had been a great support for him since Wendy abandoned him—abandoned them all—but Jace didn't want to get into the particulars of his self-loathing.

"Not everyone is Wendy," Tom said, the sentence barely tickling Jace's eardrums. "In fact, there are very few women like Wendy." Somehow his brother always knew exactly what to say, and though Jace wanted to believe him, he couldn't quite get there. Maybe because the only two women he'd ever let into his life had disappeared without a word. Just left.

Yes, there must be something seriously wrong with Jace to make his mother leave him the way she had, to make Wendy get in her car and drive to LA instead of coming to the church to get married to him.

Something was seriously wrong. He just didn't know what it was. Lately, he'd taken to thinking it was *all* him and that he'd be better off living his solitary life in the foreman's cabin for the rest of his days.

Recommitted to that goal, despite Belle's reappearance in his life, Jace was able to finish dinner with his brother and return to his lonely, isolated cabin.

CHAPTER 3

*a*nnoyance ripped through Jace as he drove into Gold Valley for the second time in as many days. Church yesterday had been a solemn affair, as one of the town's longtime residents had passed away on Friday. Jace had returned to the ranch more depressed than when he'd left.

He really hoped he wouldn't be repeating that today. Belle had insisted they meet at her office to begin picking out paint colors and flooring and window treatments. He didn't even know what a window treatment was. Why couldn't she just say curtains?

He pulled his truck into a lot filled with shiny sedans with letters for names. He couldn't fathom how they stayed so clean with all the snow, salt, and muck. His truck stood out like a sore thumb, and he vowed never to agree to meet at her office again.

In fact, he'd been toying with an idea since his dinner

with Tom. Jace didn't have to personally oversee the renovation. He just had to make sure it got done right. He could assign someone else to do the legwork, check the numbers, all of it. Landon was the obvious choice, as he knew both Jace and Gloria well enough to make intelligent decisions.

When the elevator spit him out on the fifth floor, Jace wanted to get right back inside and flee. The floor opened up to a large space filled with desks—and people. People wearing expensive suits and talking in low voices as they fingered fabrics. People leaning over computer screens together and pointing at things as decisions were made.

He took one step backward, prepared to flee. Landon would be handling the interior design from now on. That way, Jace could get back to doing what he knew how to do: ranching.

"Hey, you made it." Belle swept into his personal space and handed him a four-inch binder. "We'll start with flooring and paint today. That will really determine the rest of the textiles anyway." She didn't stop moving or talking, leaving him to follow in her wake as she carved a path through the bodies and desks to one near the wall. Thankfully, the nearest people sat about fifteen feet away.

Jace didn't understand his panic. He'd been in crowds before—church yesterday had been a complete circus. He'd been grateful, actually, because then he got lost in the chaos and didn't have to talk to anyone.

But here, now, the walls pressed too close, way too close, and the people spoke so loud, so loud. Too much noise. His heart slammed against his breastbone, seeking release.

Sweat broke out under the band of his hat. His chest tightened, the way it had when he'd attempted to go to college ten years ago.

He hadn't been able to handle the pressure then, and it felt twice as heavy right now.

Eventually, he found Belle staring at him, her phone pressed to her ear. Worry rode in the depths of her eyes, and tension tightened her mouth. He heard her say, "Panic attack?" and then, "What should I do, Tom?"

Jace took a big breath—or tried to. It felt like he was trying to suck air through a straw. He held up his hand like he just needed one more moment and closed his eyes.

He definitely wouldn't be returning to this office. In fact, if he never saw Belle again, that would be just fine by him.

———

Belle kept Tom on the line for a few more minutes, asking him questions the man wouldn't answer. He just kept saying, "It'll pass, and then Jace'll tell you everything." She finally hung up, but Jace still hadn't fully recovered.

His skin looked waxy and gray—her first indication that something was wrong. When he started gasping for air, she'd wanted to call 9-1-1. But when she went to dial, her fingers found his brother's number and called him instead.

She gave Jace silence and space while the color seeped back into his face, while his chest rose and fell evenly, while he wiped the sweat from his forehead. Belle felt like throwing up. What had caused Jace—a seemingly strong, healthy, smart man—to have a panic attack? When did he start having those? And why?

Her curiosity and compassion fully piqued, Belle simply watched him. She should probably have an attack of her own—if he found out the firm wasn't really a firm at all, but a conglomerate that allowed independent designers access to cheaper suppliers and discounted materials, he'd be furious.

They wouldn't back her if she messed up. They took a percentage of her commission in exchange for office space and access to tradesmen and wholesalers. Her job was to bring in new accounts so the conglomerate continued to make money. The seven-hundred-fifty-thousand price-tag at Horseshoe Home had been the largest account so far this month, and she couldn't lose it.

So she'd signed her name on his contract and promised herself she wouldn't deliver anything but exactly what he wanted. Then questions would never be asked. The sticky point of the firm would never be known.

Her phone buzzed, and she glanced at it. The woman from the hotel. Her fingers itched to take the call, and Jace still hadn't opened his eyes.

"Excuse me," she said as quietly as she could. She swiped open the call as she stepped away. "Tilly, good to hear from you."

"We loved your portfolio, Belle. When can you come meet with us?"

"How about this afternoon?" She glanced back to the still frozen Jace. Would they be finished by lunchtime?

"One o'clock would work. Check-in is at three, and we can work until then."

"One o'clock it is." She hoped her smile had infused the words, because by the time she turned back to her desk, it had vanished.

So had Jace.

CHAPTER 4

*B*elle felt like she'd been kicked by a horse. And she knew the feeling, because her treasured Strawberry Shortcake, a red-haired mare, had once kicked her in the chest when she'd gotten spooked.

She glanced around, frantically trying to find him among the groups lingering in the office. She caught sight of his black cowboy hat just as the elevator doors closed behind him. Leaping into action, she hurried toward the stairs. For perhaps the first time in her life, she thanked the Lord for her height, because it meant she never wore heels. And certainly she could beat an elevator down five flights of steps in her ballet flats.

Okay, she totally couldn't. By the time she burst into the lobby, panting and with her hair plastered to her face, a couple of people were loading into the already-empty elevator. Her gaze flew to the exit, where she saw Jace adjusting his hat and zipping his coat.

"Jace!"

He heard her; she saw those powerful shoulders flinch; but he didn't turn back. Just pushed open the door and stepped through it. Cursing the fact that she'd left her coat upstairs, Belle hustled after him.

"Jace, I know you can hear me. Where are you going?"

"Back to the ranch." His stride didn't slow or shorten.

She ran to catch him, nearly going down on a slick patch of ice on the sidewalk. She reached him as he arrived at his truck. "We haven't done anything yet."

He pierced her with a dark-eyed glare. "I can't do this," he said. "I'm gonna have Landon handle the reno." He got in his truck and started it. If she didn't want to get hit, she had no choice but to fall back and let him go.

She fumed as she stomped back up to her desk. Didn't he understand what was at stake for her?

Of course he doesn't, she thought. *How could he?*

Just like she didn't know why he had panic attacks. She didn't want to talk about her failures in California and she suspected Jace had a few secrets in his past too. She couldn't fault him for that.

Once inside the warmth of the building, she called Landon. Of course he didn't answer. He never did during the day. Jace probably had some asinine policy about cell phone usage while shoveling out horse stalls. Didn't he know the world ran on cell phones these days?

She hung up without leaving a message. Jace hadn't talked to Landon yet. Belle's chest felt hollow and tight. She needed Horseshoe Home's account. She couldn't lose it because of Jace's baggage or whatever had caused him to freeze up at her desk.

She dialed him, surprised when he picked up after only one ring. "Let's go get something to eat," she said before he could do anything but say, "Hello."

"My treat. No samples. I just want to find out what style you want. We'll just talk." She held her breath after her rushed sentence. In the background, she heard air blowing and the low warble of the radio. At least he hadn't hung up.

"I only have until one o'clock," she continued.

"You want to talk to me for four hours?"

"No." Her mind spun. "Just...however long it takes to eat. Where do you want to go?" She'd be lucky if she could force down more than water, but she pressed her lips together. Now was not the time for her tongue to get in her way.

"Bear Paw Café," he said, and the line went dead.

Belle stared at the phone in her hand, unsure if she should throw it to the floor and watch it shatter into a million pieces or calmly slide it into her skirt pocket. She could return to her desk and prep for her meeting with Tilly. Forget about Jace Lovell and how frustrated he made her. She headed for the elevator, still debating with herself.

She stood at her desk, her mind circling, circling. Finally, she reached for her coat, slipped it on, and headed downstairs to the parking lot.

————

Jace sipped black coffee in the corner booth at the Bear Paw Café. He saw Belle enter and glance around. Her gaze swept right over him, making his heart clench at the same time his stomach revolted against the hot liquid he'd consumed.

He hadn't been able to pinpoint why being in her office had caused him to panic, but he knew someone as smart and savvy as Belle would require an explanation. He'd swerved into the café's parking lot while on the phone with her, and then he'd immediately called Tom. After being reassured that Tom hadn't told Belle anything, Jace had gone inside and asked for the corner booth. This late on a Monday morning in the dead of winter, it hadn't been hard to get.

Finally, the hostess pointed toward him in the corner and he lifted his hand to acknowledge that Belle should come over. She glided toward him with all the grace of a beauty queen, another fact that made Jace wilt.

"I won't lie. I'm surprised you're here." Belle slid into the booth and unceremoniously deposited her purse next to her on the seat. "I was gonna be so mad if you'd told me to come here and then you'd skipped town." Her green eyes blazed, and Jace only hated himself a little bit for enjoying getting her fired up.

He wanted to snap back at her with something witty and charmingly cruel. But all that came out of his mouth was, "Sorry, Belle."

She studied him, her eyes narrowing the teensiest bit. He squirmed and ducked his head to give himself some protection with his cowboy hat. "Stop that."

"Just tryin' to figure you out."

"Look who's talkin' like a cowboy now." He glanced up and quirked a smile at her. "And I don't need to be figured out." Although, if someone would try, he'd want it to be Belle. He nearly slopped hot coffee on his hand with this thought, so he set the mug down. "You wanna eat?" He flagged down the waitress.

Belle ordered coffee and the Western omelet. Jace opted for the French toast with hashbrowns, and the waitress left them alone again. Words crowded the back of his throat.

"My fiancé left me at the altar seven months ago," he blurted out. "Sometimes I…I don't do well in situations and places I can't control." At least that was what the psychiatrist had told him. Jace wasn't sure if that was why he'd panicked in Belle's office or not, but the explanation appeased her.

Made her sympathetic, even. Her eyes glittered now, this time with compassion. "I'm so sorry, Jace." Her hands came across the table and touched his for a heartbeat. She yanked them back like she'd been singed by his skin, and he ducked his head again.

He'd definitely been burned by her touch. The heat of it traveled through his arms, across his shoulders, and down into his gut. The silence descending on them felt tangible, thick, terrible.

He cleared his throat. "I'm doin' okay these days." He lifted his eyes to hers. "Most days. Today's just not one of them."

She'd leaned way back in the booth, positioning herself as far from him as she could get. "But you're okay here?"

He glanced away, out the window. The bright sun on the snow nearly blinded him. "I like the corner booth."

Several moments passed in silence. "You're a mystery," she finally said. The waitress brought her coffee and she stirred cream and sugar into it while she watched him. "So, tell me what you're looking for in the cowboy cabins."

Jace seized onto the easy topic, though he wished he had someone like Belle he could confess to, spill his secrets to, speak with about the ghosts that haunted him. She hadn't seemed judgmental of Wendy abandoning him on their wedding day. Maybe—

"Did I lose you again?" Belle leaned forward and peered at him.

"You shouldn't wear so much makeup," he said. "Can't see your freckles."

She fell back again like he'd punched her. She blinked, and her mouth opened, but she only said, "You like freckles?"

"A face is sort of a waste without them." He lifted his coffee to his lips, wondering what he was saying. How had this conversation gone so badly, so quickly? He forced himself to focus. "The cowboys need updated appliances and carpet that's easy to take care of but can weather a lot of boot traffic. They need neutral colors on the walls and comfortable, sturdy furniture. They work really hard for long hours. Their cabin should be an escape from that."

She nodded as the waitress arrived with their food. "What colors are neutral to you?"

"Gray, or I don't know." Jace smeared the butter on his

French toast. "Eggshell, or whatever you fancy designers call it."

"Not white."

"Shows too much dirt," he said. "And we get dirty."

"Oh, I've seen how dirty you get."

Jace chuckled, his spirits lifting a little bit with the easy banter of the beautiful woman across from him. "The cabins have exposed wood in the ceiling. That can stay. We do live on a ranch."

"Maybe it just needs to be refreshed?" Belle forked a bite of omelet into her mouth. "Dark stain would offset well with eggshell. Or gray."

Jace noticed her hopeful expression, the nervous tick of her eyes as she looked into his. He didn't know what to make of it. "You can come see my place," he said. "It's bigger than the rest, but the color scheme and wood beams are similar."

A rosy flush colored her fair cheeks. "You inviting me to your house?"

"Or maybe you've already been to Landon's cabin." Jace couldn't sort through how he felt. He definitely wanted Belle to come to his house. But at the same time, his cabin provided the only sanctuary he had left. If she entered it… Jace didn't know what would happen. And that scared him.

"I haven't been to Landon's."

"No? No brother-sister-bonding time?"

"He comes to the house sometimes."

Jace noticed she didn't say *my house*. "You plannin' on staying in town long?"

She picked at her food, moving ham and tomatoes around without eating anything. "I—I'm not sure."

"Your parents will be gone for six more months."

"This job could take that long, I suppose."

"And then you'll go?" He wasn't sure why he cared so much, but he yearned to know.

She flashed him an annoyed glare. "I don't know."

"Okay, okay." He tried on a smile but it felt wrong, so he wiped it away.

"Tell me about the lodge. Who works there, what kind of things you do there, that sort of thing."

Jace liked the tonalities of her voice, the way she watched him with rapt attention when he spoke, how she didn't write anything down. So he allowed himself to relax and get lost in telling her about the ranch. By the time he finished, Belle rushed off to her next appointment, and Jace realized he'd been talking for hours.

It felt good.

CHAPTER 5

*J*ace aimed his truck under the arch boasting the double-H logo, and everything in his chest released as he drove onto the ranch. He drove down the road and around the bend, where the homestead sat on the left side of the road, and the inner workings of the ranch—the lodge, the barns, stables, silos, and the long row of cowboy cabins, with Tom's way down at the end, ran along the right side.

When Landon exited the administration trailer—without a coat—and headed toward him before he'd gotten out of his truck, Jace quickened his pace. "What's wrong?"

"Sent Ty and Nelson out to the west fence this morning. They were gonna de-ice the fence line, reset the posts, and be back by lunch."

"Right." Jace didn't like the worried lines around Landon's eyes.

"They didn't come back. We can't reach them on the radio."

Jace checked his watch. Quarter to two. They should've been back three hours ago. "Did you send anyone out there?"

"Rob went with Elliot."

"Rob went?" The owner of Horseshoe Home got involved with dealings on the ranch from time to time, but usually nothing more than giving out bonuses or boosting morale.

"He insisted. He happened to be in the office when I realized they hadn't come back in yet."

"When did we realize it?"

"Well, Gloria brought lunch, so...." Landon frowned at the ground. "They only left about one o'clock."

"They have radios?"

Landon held up the handheld device as an answer. Jace took it, and pressed the button. "Rob, come in, Rob. It's Jace."

The silence unnerved him. Not only the silence from the radio, but that pressing on him from all sides. The Montana winter snows could do that—mute everything until the quiet drove a man mad.

"Jace," came through the radio.

"Where you at?" Jace asked.

"Almost to the fence site," Rob said. "I'll keep you posted."

"How long?"

"'Bout ten minutes."

Jace confirmed that he expected to hear in ten minutes and gestured for Landon to come with him into the lodge. "Where are the rest of the boys?"

"Stables or barn. I gave them all something to do, what with the sun shining and all. Didn't see any point in hanging around here, worrying."

"Good call, Landon." Jace clapped him on the back as they went inside. Jace had never noticed the things the building lacked, but after talking to Belle—and being in that beautiful building where she worked—he saw all the flaws. He ignored them as he strode toward his office, guilt gripping his gut. He should've been here—at the ranch where he belonged—not enjoying breakfast with Belle.

Just another reason to pass the renovation on to Landon. Then Jace could continue to manage the ranch.

Twelve minutes passed while Jace beat himself up for being absent when his men needed him. Twelve minutes before the radio made another noise. "Jace, come back."

"Jace here. Landon's with me."

"We made it to the work site. They've been here, but they're not here now."

Jace heaved a sigh and closed his eyes. He prayed for the safety of his cowboys, his friends. "I'll call emergency services."

"We'll follow the tracks. We didn't see anything on the way in."

"Keep the radio on," Jace said. The conversation ended, and Jace looked at Landon for several long seconds. "I should've been here."

"Nothin' you coulda done different."

"I might have noticed they were gone sooner."

Landon swallowed, his green eyes bright with defiance. So much like Belle's, but they didn't elicit the same emotion in Jace that hers did.

"I didn't mean that," Jace said. "You're a good cowboy, Landon." He stood and moved to the landline in the front of the building to call the authorities. They might send an ambulance out. They might not. Jace didn't really know what to expect, but it was standard procedure to let the authorities know when men went missing on the ranch.

Jace and Landon then moved some chairs to face the windows so they could keep a vigil until their friends returned.

———

Belle's phone rang just as she sat down to eat the salad she'd brought home. Jace's face brightened the screen, brightened the room, brightened her life. She smiled before she could remember that he rubbed her the wrong way, that he was a cowboy, her brother's friend, and well, *Jace*.

"Hello?" She acted like she didn't know who was calling.

"Hey." Jace sounded tired. "You talked to Landon yet?"

"Haven't heard from him. Why?" Something in his voice concerned her, made her forget about the deliciousness she'd brought home.

"We had some trouble out at the ranch today. He was pretty upset by the end of it."

"What happened?"

"Lost some of our men for a little while. We found them, but Landon feels responsible. I told him he wasn't, but...he said he didn't want to stay in his cabin. See, one of the men who was stuck out in the cold is his roommate. The paramedics took both men to the hospital, just to make sure they're okay."

Belle got up and moved to the front window, as if she'd see her brother coming up the sidewalk at any moment. "How long ago did he leave?"

"Coupla hours. I told him to call me when he got to your place. He hasn't checked in."

"Jace." Belle took a deep breath and tried to reason through her rising anxiety. "He hasn't called. And he hasn't been here."

"You sure he's not there? How long have you been home?"

She stepped away from the window and headed toward the bedrooms on the left side of the house. "Only about ten minutes, but I'd have seen his truck." She opened all the doors. Her brother wasn't there. "Where could he have gone?"

She headed downstairs, but it sat empty too. She even checked the backyard while Jace attempted to soothe her. He finally said, "I'll come pick you up. We'll check his usual haunts."

"I'll call him," Belle said, the only thing she could think to do while she waited for Jace to make the thirty-minute drive from the ranch.

"See you soon."

Belle hung up and dialed Landon. He answered on the first ring. "Where are you?" she demanded, equal parts relief and rage roiling through her. Loud music pounded through the line. "Why didn't you check in with Jace?"

"Did he call you?"

"He's worried about you. Of course he called me. And I've been freaking out for five minutes while he explained everything." She took a deep breath and ran her hand through her hair. "Come home, okay?"

"Sorry, Belle." He sounded sincere.

"I'll call Jace. He's on his way here."

"Tell him I'm sorry too."

Belle agreed and hung up. She tried Jace, but he didn't answer. She wondered how he had service at the ranch in the first place. She hadn't been able to receive texts.

Landon arrived at the house and Belle hugged him tight. "It's not your fault. Accidents happen."

"Don't want to talk about it." His eyes seemed darker and more dangerous than Belle had ever remembered seeing them.

"Okay." She gestured toward the freezer. "I have ice cream."

He pulled open the door. "Perfect." He took out the container and scooped up a dishful of chocolate. Belle tried Jace again, with no success.

He arrived at the house five minutes after Landon fell asleep in the living room, the TV blaring and his empty bowl in front of him on the coffee table.

Belle let him in and gestured him into the formal living room. "He was just at the sport's bar," she whispered. "He's fine."

"Is he?" Jace tried to look over her shoulder, but he couldn't see around the corner.

"He's clammed up." Belle rubbed her hands up and down her arms. "Didn't want to talk about it. I tried to call you."

"I saw when I got out of the canyon. I figured I was already almost here. So…." He seemed to realize how close they stood at the same time she did. He backed up a step, meeting the desk behind him, as she retreated into the hall.

She couldn't look away from him. His gaze bored into hers as well, creating an electric circuit between them. She shook her head, trying to get the attraction between them to settle down a notch. Plus, she had no idea what her body was doing, finding him so desirable, so alluring.

"Are you still gonna make him do the renovation?" she asked, her voice straying up into another octave. "You know, he has no taste."

"You think I do?" Jace took a small step forward, enough for the light in the hall to illuminate his smoldering eyes and catch on the edge of his jaw.

Belle licked her lips; her eyes traced the edges of his beard. "More than him."

Jace dipped his head, hiding that handsome face. A sense of loss Belle didn't understand rang through her. "I don't know, Belle."

A thrill ran through her when he said her name. "Why not?"

"If I'd been there today instead of meetin' with you, I might have noticed those men were gone sooner."

"Where were they?"

"They fixed the fence and had started to come back in. But their vehicle got stuck in the snow and when they tried to get it out, it rolled down the embankment. Ruined their radio. They then hiked three miles through the snow to a cabin we have out on the property. They built a fire and dug in." He inched forward again. "Landon couldn't have done anything more than he did."

"Neither could you," she said, lifting her chin. If he stepped closer, drew his arm around her waist, and leaned down, she could kiss him. Her gaze focused on his mouth, and she lost all reason as she fantasized about what it would be like to touch her lips to his.

"I'll call you tomorrow." He swept by her without touching her, though the heat from his body made her tremble. He checked on Landon, who snored softly on the sofa. Jace came back, and he brushed his fingers against hers for the briefest of moments. A whisper almost, barely tangible and barely there. She tried to hold on, but his fingers disappeared.

"I'll let you know if I can do the renovation tomorrow, okay?" His breath coasted over her shoulder, slid down her spine. She couldn't speak, so she simply nodded and Jace let himself out.

Belle braced herself against the doorway and breathed. What was going on? She hadn't been so attracted to a man since, well, she'd never been so attracted to a man. Even her last boyfriend didn't hold a candle to the electricity that had flowed between her and Jace just now.

She pushed her ex from her mind. She didn't need bad memories and her poisoned past haunting her, not right now. No, all she wanted to do was stand where Jace had so she could smell his cologne. A smile played with her lips as she thought about working with him on the renovations, beside him, day after day.

Please help him believe he can work with me, she prayed.

———

Belle suffered through her morning of organizing suppliers for Tilly and the hotel. The woman was stuck in the eighties, but Belle knew just how to bring her into the future. She'd made a list as soon as she'd arrived at her desk, and now four binders lay open in front of her, product numbers recorded and prices checked online. Belle enjoyed the work —there was something about making lists and checking things off that appealed to her. Sometimes she even made lists of things she'd already done, just so she could experience the rush of accomplishment when she crossed off the items.

It was a sickness, really. As was watching the clock on her computer. The minutes seemed to tick by. She glanced down, noticed her phone face-down on her desk, and flipped it over with an edge of panic in her motions.

What if she'd missed Jace's call?

But she hadn't. Her black screen stared back at her,

reflecting her auburn hair and making her eyes look like dark pits. She unconsciously ran her fingers through her hair and tucked it behind her ear. As a child, she'd longed to have a normal hair color. Anything but the dark red that seemed to catch everyone's attention—and not in a good way.

She sighed and pushed her first-world problems away. She could dye her hair if she really wanted to. But the upkeep took too much money and too much time, both luxuries Belle didn't have in Gold Valley. In Sacramento, before she'd been blamed for the Mix-Up of the Century, sure. But now? Definitely not.

Her phone buzzed and the ringtone began to play. Her heart kicked out a series of extra beats, but it was only Calvin.

"Hey, Calvin."

"You should answer the phone with a, 'Good morning. This is Belle Edmunds. How can I help you?'" The disdain in his voice practically dripped from the phone.

"I knew it was you."

"I see the Rimrod Lodge hired you."

Pride swelled in Belle's chest and leaked into her voice when she said, "Yes. I got the paperwork signed yesterday."

"I have another lead for you."

Her suspicions went up. "For me? You don't want the client?"

"I'm far too busy for something like this." He acted like he designed castles for kings.

Belle employed her professionalism, glad for maybe the

first time for her tutelage in Sacramento. There, she'd been nothing but perfect, nothing but professional, at all times. By the time she returned to her apartment each evening, she'd been utterly spent.

"Who is it, Calvin?"

"The Flathead Lake Hotel and Spa."

Belle frowned. "Flathead Lake is, what? Two hours from here?" The thought of driving around the mountain and across the Flathead Reservation—during the height of winter—made Belle shiver.

"About two hours, yes," Calvin confirmed. "It's a million-dollar contract. They want a complete overhaul, from top to bottom."

"Right now? Isn't the lake frozen?"

"They just barely put out the job. It could be a few months before it starts."

"Good," Belle said. "I don't think I can handle Horseshoe Home, Rimrod Lodge, and driving to Flathead Lake every other day." She'd only ordered materials for a few clients in Sacramento. Never more than one at a time—usually. The job that had been botched in California had been one of three clients she'd ordered for in the same day.

She hadn't made a mistake, but she'd been blamed for the barn door coming in with the absolute wrong dimensions. The designer who should've been fired that day still worked at the company, and she'd thrown Belle under the bus faster than Belle thought possible. She'd wondered since losing her apartment and returning to the mountain town of Gold Valley, if Ynes lost sleep at night because of what she'd done. Belle certainly did. She wondered if she'd stood up for herself, if things could've been different. But she hadn't. She'd been trained to be a silent bystander and that was how she went out.

"Do you want to send them your portfolio?" Calvin's snappy tone erased the past from Belle's mind.

"Yeah, I mean, yes. When is the proposal due?" She glanced at the binders on her desk and wondered if she really wanted another client right now. *A million dollar contract*, her mind whispered.

With a contract like that, Belle could leave the conglomerate and start her own business. Never mind that she had no home of her own in Gold Valley. She wasn't tied to the area, though she loved the naturally occurring waterfalls and the soothing sound of the river at night.

"Not until the end of February," Calvin said, pulling her back to the proposal. "They're casting a wide net on this one, but I think having someone close, someone who knows Montana, will give you an edge."

"Thanks, Calvin." Belle hung up. The minutes blurred into hours, and still Jace hadn't called. Belle toyed with the idea of calling him herself, but she didn't trust herself not to demand that he tell her what he'd decided about working with her on the reno.

She didn't want to hear him say he couldn't. The silence meant she could still hope that he would decide to work with her on the ranch.

After she arrived at home, she made herself a BLT salad and went down the hall to her bedroom to eat. The house seemed to swallow her. Overlarge for just one person, Belle felt safest in her bedroom.

She'd just started to doze when her phone rang. Jace's name on her screen made anticipation skip into adrenaline.

"Hey," she said. "It's about time you called. I've been thinking about you all day." As soon as her sentence ended, she realized what she'd said.

"You have, have you?" He chuckled. "Well, that's nice to hear."

"Not like that," she hurried to add, though if she were being honest, there was a little fantasizing about him mixed in with the desperation and worry that he'd choose to assign Landon to the reno.

"Like what then?"

"Are you going to work with me or not?"

"Well, when you ask like that, I'm not so sure."

"Jace."

"Belle."

"You're a stubborn man."

"And you're fun to tease."

"I was asleep, you know."

"Asleep?" Disbelief tainted his voice. "Belle, it's seven-thirty."

"I know what time it is."

"Will we need to go to dinner before four o'clock to get the early-bird special?" He laughed, this time a full laugh she didn't recognize.

"They wouldn't let your baby face in," she said.

"But we can go to dinner, right?"

"Tonight? I already ate." Her brain ran on overdrive, trying to figure out what he was asking.

"How 'bout tomorrow, then?"

"Jace, are you gonna work with me or assign Landon to the reno?"

"You'll have to wait until dinner tomorrow to find out."

"Jace."

"I'll swing by your office at three-thirty. Or will that be too late? Want to make sure I get you home in enough time to get your beauty rest."

"I don't need beauty rest," she snapped.

"You're right about that, sunshine."

Belle's brain tripped. She couldn't think. Nothing came out of her mouth. "Are you calling me pretty?"

"I probably would've used beautiful. But pretty works."

"Sunshine?" Her mind had just caught up to that part of what he'd said.

"Belle, I have to go. My brother just walked in." He hung up before she could say another word. She took the phone from her ear and stared at it as the call disconnected. What in the world was going on?

CHAPTER 6

*J*ace paced in his living room. His empty living room. He had no idea where Tom was and he said, "Please forgive me for lyin'," as he spun on his heel and headed back the way he'd come.

He had no idea where the words he'd spoken had come from. Had he really invited Belle to dinner? Called her beautiful? Given her a *pet name*?

He groaned, flopped onto the couch, and ran his hands over his face. He'd just wanted to let her know that he'd decided to play point on the renovation. Number one, he didn't have a whole lot to do in the winter. Number two, well, every number after one was filled with the fact that he liked Belle.

There, he'd admitted it. He liked Belle Edmunds. He liked her smile. He liked the sound of her voice over the phone. He liked the sweet perfume she wore.

Another guttural noise tore from his mouth. He couldn't

believe he was even considering another relationship. After Wendy, well, he didn't think he'd ever want another woman in his life. He wrestled with what he wanted for the rest of the evening, most of the night, and all the way through breakfast.

And he still didn't know.

He left the ranch in the capable hands of Landon—who lounged in the large room with a dozen other cowboys, watching episode after episode of some sitcom—and drove into town. This time when he parked in front of Belle's building, he felt no tightening in his chest. No shortness of breath. Nothing.

He still didn't quite understand why he'd reacted the way he had. At three-thirty, he texted her, and a few minutes later, she emerged from the building. He watched her strut toward him, her long skirt almost dragging on the sidewalk. She looked sophisticated wearing all black, with that bright yellow purse draped over her forearm. Jace glanced down at his jeans and leather jacket. She outclassed him in every sense of the word.

She flashed a smile and climbed into the truck. "Where are we going to dinner?"

"Only the buffet gives senior citizen discounts."

"Better be prepared to get carded."

"You really think I have a baby face?"

She stared at him for what seemed like a long time. Long enough for him to maneuver through the lot to the exit. Long enough for him to turn into traffic. Long enough to make him squirm.

"Nah, I guess not."

"Sorry I called you pretty." His fingers clenched. "I mean—"

"You're sorry you called me pretty?"

"I just mean—"

She waited for him to go on, but he had no idea what to say. "Landon has too much to do on the ranch. I'll be working with you."

The sun didn't stand a chance next to her beaming face. "That's great."

They arrived at the buffet and Jace offered Belle his arm as they started toward the entrance. Thankfully, she took it. The mere weight of her arm in his made his blood flow faster. He held open the door with one hand and slipped his fingers into hers.

Her eyes locked with his, and he squeezed her hand before releasing it. In that single breath, he'd seen what he needed to.

Sure, Jace liked Belle.

And she liked him too.

———

"I'm heading into the valley." Jace shrugged into his coat as he passed Landon's desk.

"Again?"

A sigh escaped his lips though Jace tried to hold it in. "Yeah. Apparently, my opinion on the carpet is *necessary*." Belle had insisted he accompany her on every shopping trip, preview every paint color, authorize every purchase. The first week it had been cute, enjoyable even.

Now, as the end of the second week approached, driving into town felt like a chore. But he did have an inexplicable urge to see Belle, hold her hand—which she'd let him do several times as they wandered through huge warehouses full of furnishings—and breathe in her calming scent.

He didn't dare do much more than twine his fingers with hers. He didn't put his arm around her. He didn't walk her to the door. He didn't ask her out beyond their work excursions. He wanted to, but he couldn't. Some invisible force held him back, pushed against his desire to start a new relationship.

He knew what that force was. Wendy Suman. The woman had ruined him, and Jace didn't trust himself to make smart decisions when it came to dating. The fact that he wanted to get to know Belle also unsettled him. He'd known her for years and had never once looked at her the way he was now. In fact, he'd never even gotten along all that great with her. Everything in his world felt upside down, and he was still trying to figure out how to move forward.

Belle met him on the curb—she always did—or at a specified location. He hadn't told her he didn't want to come back up to her office, but she had a sixth sense about such things.

"Morning," she said as she adjusted her seat belt.

"Mornin'."

"So I've found three carpets I think would work." She glanced at him, and she seemed nervous.

"Okay." He turned onto the street and enjoyed the frozen-over river out his window. A strong sense of nostalgia engulfed him, reminding him of how much he loved Montana, even in the thick of January.

Jace whistled to himself as they drove, as Belle directed him toward the warehouse where he'd spent yesterday afternoon. At least it was heated. "Couldn't we have looked at these yesterday?"

Belle looked at him as she slid out of the truck, her eyes wide and round. "Am I taking you from your work on the ranch?"

"Yep." He rounded the truck and hooked his arm through hers. "But it's okay. You're not the worst company I've had today."

"Oh, that's so comforting. I know the kind of riffraff you hang out with."

"Landon is riffraff? What does that make you? And who says riffraff?" He laughed, enjoying the feeling all the way down to his cowboy boots. He hadn't laughed in a really long time. Truly laughed at something he found funny.

In truth, he hadn't *lived* in a really long time. "Thanks for inviting me," he said. "I do want to see the carpets."

"You do not." Her pace increased, but Jace had long legs too.

"I do. It's better than submitting paperwork for paychecks."

"You seemed kind of upset."

"Not upset." He opened the door and she entered in front of him. He sidled up next to her, but kept his hands to himself. "Just...do you bring all your clients to pick out every aspect of their project?"

She didn't, and she didn't even have to say anything for him to know. He could read it on her face. "Why you askin' me to come along all the time?"

She swallowed, took several more steps. "Look, you're my first client since—" Her lips pressed together and her already-fair complexion turned almost transparent.

"Since what?"

"Since nothing." She glanced around and seized upon the first person she saw—a janitor, from the looks of him. She made a beeline for him, leaving Jace wondering what she didn't want him to know.

He wouldn't get her to tell him, he knew that. The woman was determined if nothing else. So the next two hours became hyper-focused on carpets, and pilling, and fibers, and other things Jace didn't know and didn't care about.

When Belle asked him to lunch, surprise shot through Jace. He wasn't sure why. He'd seen the edge in her eyes. But still, he didn't see himself as someone who would interest a woman like Belle. He wanted to ask her what she saw in him, but they'd just started getting along.

And he did need to eat.

"Sure, lunch sounds great." He nudged her with his shoulder. "You payin'?"

"You'd make a lady pay?"

He glanced around. "Don't see a lady."

Her outraged gasp made him laugh again. When he quieted, he said, "I just see a beautiful woman. I guess I can pay for her."

A flush rose in Belle's cheeks, and she slipped her hand into his. Nothing more needed to be said.

———

Belle had no idea what she was doing. Did this strange banter count as flirting? She wasn't quite sure what else to do with Jace. With her previous boyfriend, their connection had been about the ocean, and gourmet coffees, and the client they both wanted to please. Casual dinners had become romantic quickly, and Belle could see the same thing happening with Jace.

If only she'd let it. Something inside her held her back from fully flirting with him. He obviously found her attractive, and they hadn't been fighting as much. She liked the strength of his fingers between hers, and found herself fantasizing about doing more than just holding hands. At the same time, she wasn't sure beginning a relationship with him was wise. He seemed...broken in a lot of ways, yet completely whole in others.

Having his fiancé leave him on their wedding day had to have shattered him and she didn't want to start something she couldn't finish. Not again. No, she was determined to go slow with every man, really learn more about them—and herself—before getting serious. After all, Belle had run the rat race of dating and breaking up enough times to be weary of it. Weary of her own shortcomings. Weary of dealing with conflicting feelings and trying to figure out when to reveal what information.

After all, she didn't really want Jace to know she didn't have much money. While she could probably afford lunch at the pancake house, it would definitely hit her budget for other things. At least until the commission came in for the Horseshoe Home account.

She'd already determined to save almost all of it. She was done living it up every time she got a paycheck and then pinching pennies between jobs.

"You alive over there?" Jace's question startled her out of her thoughts. "We've been sitting here for five minutes."

She glanced at him and then out the windshield. "This isn't the pancake house."

"It's lunchtime."

"You've never had breakfast for lunch?"

"Why would someone do that?"

"It's popular. In Sacramento, there are entire eateries that serve breakfast all day long."

"Eateries?" A chuckle rode in his voice. "And I don't normally do something just because it's popular."

"Are you even human? Have you never wanted pancakes for dinner?"

"No, I can honestly say I've never craved pancakes for dinner. In fact, I don't even like pancakes for breakfast."

"Now I know you're not human." She unbuckled and

reached for the door handle. "It's un-American not to like pancakes."

"Not much of a bacon fan either," he called as she slid to the ground.

She turned and gaped at him. "I think we should stop talking. Next thing you say might be something completely insane like 'I hate chocolate.'"

Jace opened his mouth, said, "I only like certain kinds of chocolate," and then laughter came out. The sound made her heart tremor with anticipation, with sheer desire. She wanted to hear that laugh everyday. She *needed* to hear it everyday.

She stumbled backward, closed the door, and smoothed down her hair. Her plan to have him come to town and participate in things she normally did herself seemed to have worked. He came when she called, and he seemed to have a good time with her as they wandered through warehouses and pored over paint chips.

She'd always known that he'd figure out that she didn't usually involve her clients this way. She'd done it partly to spend time with him, but a bigger part of her couldn't make a decision. She didn't want to make a mistake on his project. She couldn't afford to fail.

Her chest rumbled with anxiety as she stepped through the frozen parking lot. So much of her self-worth was tied up in being a good interior designer. When she'd lost her job in Sacramento, she'd lost her confidence too. She didn't know how to make decisions for a project, because she didn't want to choose the wrong item.

Inside the diner, she ordered the biggest stack of pancakes and an additional side of bacon and enjoyed the horrified look on Jace's face. He ordered a boring club sandwich with French fries. Total lunch food.

She gave him an exaggerated sigh and handed her menu to the waitress. "You can make a turkey sandwich at home."

"I learned to make pancakes when I was seven years old." He put his elbows on the table and leaned toward her. "And you just paid—well, *I* just paid—eight bucks for four of them. Seems unbelievable." He flashed her a smile that made her insides liquefy. She returned it and quickly dropped her gaze to the table.

"Why don't you like pancakes?"

Jace shifted in his seat and reached for the artificial sugar packets in the center of the table. He pinched a couple between his fingers and played with them. "For a while there, we ate pancakes for every meal. It was all I knew how to make."

Belle frowned, his mannerisms screaming a warning. "You made them?"

"After my mom left, there wasn't anyone else to cook." He cleared his throat. "Then Tom suggested we try borrowing a cookbook, so we did that. We gradually got better at cooking."

Belle's heart sped. She'd known Jace and Tom didn't live with their mother, but she hadn't known why. "Your mom... she left?"

Jace's dark eyes met Belle's, and she saw all the way into

his soul. "Up and left one day. Hardest thing I've ever been through. Well, until—" He clamped his lips together.

"Until Wendy." Belle reached for the sugar packets too, the pressure in her chest just tight enough to be uncomfortable.

"Mom came back a couple of summers ago, when my dad fell and broke his hip. It's been a slow process, but I figured out how to forgive her."

Belle abandoned the packets and found him watching her openly again. "You did?"

"Tom's had a harder time. She dropped us at school one day and never came to pick us up."

Belle didn't know what to say. "I'm sorry," couldn't adequately convey her horror at what he must've felt, what he must've gone through. And Wendy leaving him had hurt even more.

"How are things going with forgiving Wendy?" She barely gave air to the question, but she had to ask it.

Jace's eyes stormed, his jaw tightened, and Belle had her answer. "Sorry," she said quickly. "You don't have to tell me." She took a deep breath and pushed it out. "You're better than me. Someone betrayed me in Sacramento, and I haven't forgiven them." She glanced away as she realized something else. "Haven't even tried."

An image of Beau flashed through her mind. Tall, blond, surfer-boy muscles—and one of the most talented designers in California. He'd been at the company for five years before Belle arrived, and he still had the corner office she'd coveted.

Jace's warm fingers danced over hers. "Forgiveness is a hard thing."

"Is it?" She hated the press of tears lingering just beneath the surface. "You've done it."

"It took a long time." He tightened his hold on her hand. "Who do you need to forgive?"

Pure panic—and a lot of it—passed through her bloodstream. "I—no one."

Their food arrived at that very moment, causing Jace to withdraw his hand from hers. By the time she dared to look at him again, she'd slathered butter over all four of her pancakes and doused them with blackberry syrup.

His guards had snapped back into place. His eyes were guarded, his cowboy hat pulled low over his eyebrows, his attention on his food.

The only indication she got that she hadn't messed up too badly came when he said, "I can't believe you eat fruit-flavored syrup. I seriously can't think of anything more disgusting."

CHAPTER 7

*J*ace chewed on the information Belle had given him at lunch. Something had happened in Sacramento—he'd been right. She hadn't left willingly. She wasn't in Gold Valley by choice.

He wasn't sure why that information bothered him so much. Maybe because she didn't actually have a home here. After all, her parents would return in a few months, and then where would she go? Was it even worth trying to move past Wendy and open himself up for another woman to possibly leave him?

Jace's chest caved in and he took a breath to try to get it to expand properly. One thing he knew: He couldn't go through a situation like the one with Wendy again. If he fell in love with Belle, and then she left…. He couldn't even imagine how wrecked he'd be.

Better not to fall in love again, he told himself as he parked front of his cabin. He stared through the windshield and made a decision. He could work with Belle, but he couldn't date her. She had baggage from Sacramento to deal with, and he hadn't even considered forgiving Wendy for what she'd done. She hadn't asked him to, and he didn't want to give her such a precious gift.

They'd had exactly one conversation after she left, that he'd initiated. She'd said, "I hope you can understand one day," but Jace honestly didn't know how that was possible. His heart felt loaded with cement and his throat clogged with emotion.

He got out of the truck and headed up the steps to his front door. Once inside the safety of his cabin, he leaned against the door and sighed. *How do I forgive Wendy?* he asked. *Why does she get to act so badly? She doesn't deserve my forgiveness.*

He knew he should forgive her. The preacher talked about God's forgiveness as unconditional, and that man was obligated to forgive everyone. But Jace was sure his fiancé hadn't left him standing at the front of a crowd of people in favor of a lucrative real estate job in Los Angeles. Without a word, a text, any indication whatsoever. Without an apology even.

Familiar fury and frustration and foolishness flowed through him. He hated how she'd made him feel that day. No, she didn't deserve to just leave and forget him, leave and be forgiven.

You forgave your mother, his mind whispered, and Jace fisted his fingers. Life seemed so unfair. Because his mother had left, he shouldn't have had to deal with a fiancé doing the same thing. Why did he have to go through that twice? Tom had found his happy ending and all Jace had was bitter regret.

To get his mind to calm down, he marched into the kitchen and yanked open a drawer. He pulled out a couple of hand warmers and cracked them to get the chemicals to start producing heat. He sure couldn't stay here and rehash everything that had happened. If he did, he'd have to fix all the holes he'd punch into the walls.

Better to channel that anger into productive work, and he was sure there was something on the ranch that needed to be done. Something no one else wanted to do.

But Jace would do it. Good, old dependable Jace, who thought it better to dedicate himself to a ranch than to a woman. At least the ranch would never leave him.

———

Belle didn't call and request his presence to pick out countertops or curtains for a solid week. He saw her at church, but she sat with Landon, and Jace didn't want his cowhand to know that he'd held his sister's hand. Belle hadn't said anything to Landon either, or Jace would've had the cowboy in his face at the ranch.

He didn't call her or text her either. His decision made, Jace intended to keep to himself until he could figure out how to move on. He was determined to keep things professional between them.

So when his phone buzzed on Thursday morning while

he processed the payroll, surprise shot through him to see her name attached to a text.

We'll be ready to paint on Monday. Does that work for the ranch?

She didn't ask if it worked for *him*, and the difference wasn't lost on Jace. A pinch started behind his eyes, and he focused on his work instead of answering her. She could wait.

He didn't make her wait long. Just wasn't in him, he supposed. *Monday's fine. What do I need to do to be ready for the painters?*

We'll start in the lodge. Just try to move all the furniture away from the walls.

Sure thing. He'd just finished his text when Landon poked his head into the office. "Walt and Ty just got back, and they need to see you."

Jace stood without questioning Landon. He'd sent Walt and Ty out to feed the herd—a task that required using tractors and hauling hay for hours—and he knew their tractors needed maintenance. He'd spent his rage in the equipment bay for hours when he'd been trying to work through his feelings for Belle.

"Something with the tractor?" he asked when he met the pair only a couple of steps down the hallway.

Ty, a tall, dark-haired man in his mid-twenties glanced at Walt, his senior by a decade. The man had been in business before leaving it for the slower life on a ranch. He'd learned the work was just as never-ending, but in a different way.

"She got stuck, like we knew she would." He exchanged a glance with Ty. "We were a little aggressive getting 'er out, and well, we mowed over a fence."

Alarms rang in Jace's ears. "The cattle?"

"We need all hands on deck," Ty said. "Several boys already went out to try to keep the ones that are still contained inside the fences. But some are loose."

Jace hurried back to his office and grabbed his coat. "How many are loose?" He swiped the radio from his desk.

"Couple dozen," Ty said. "Sorry, boss."

"Don't be sorry. Let's just round 'em up." Jace led the way out of the lodge and into the nearly frozen air. "Why didn't someone just radio in?"

"We did, boss. You didn't answer. That's why we sent Landon in to get you. Wasn't sure what was goin' on."

Jace frowned at the radio, but as he rounded the building and faced the paddocks where they kept the cows in the winter, his attention got swept away by the chaos before him. He spent months getting the cows comfortable around humans, but now scared cattle lowed from near barns and other places they deemed safe.

A dozen men, including Rob, swarmed around the site of the accident. No one seemed to be doing anything, though.

"Boys!" Jace called as he strode forward. "Half of you go get your lassos. Ty, Caleb, Tucker, Paul, Wade, and Walt." He rattled names off in an authoritative tone. "The rest of you get rope from the barn and let's get this tractor out of here.

Landon, fetch me one, will you? Rob and I will keep the cows inside."

The weathered owner looked at him and nodded, his eyes shining with the same emotion dancing through Jace: Excitement.

Winter held only the promise of boring chores—in bitter temperatures—on the ranch. Prepping for breeding, for calving, for planting. Paying men to feed thousands of cows. Dealing with thousands of cows and their nutritional needs.

Yes, a stuck tractor, a broken fence, and loose cattle definitely added spice to Jace's predictable day, and he wasn't at all sorry about it.

———

Belle skipped church on Sunday. When Landon texted her and asked why she wasn't there, she told him she wasn't feeling well. It wasn't entirely a lie. The thought of seeing Jace tomorrow morning at the ranch had kept her stomach in knots since she'd texted him on Thursday.

His response had seemed casual, but she couldn't tell much through a text. She knew their communication had come to a screeching halt after that fateful lunch. She'd quit working on his project, instead focusing on her proposal for the Flathead Lake Hotel and then meeting with Tilly about her needs at the lodge. She'd set up painters for Horseshoe Home, and that should take several weeks to get all the cabins and the lodge done.

So instead of going to church—where she'd just avoid

Jace—she paced in her kitchen, her mind churning over what she'd do to the house if it were hers to remodel. She closed her eyes and imagined it as a blank canvas where she could add her personal touch.

These thoughts calmed her, the way they always did. Designing was the only thing that ever could. She had another reason for skipping church too—she didn't want to continue pondering how she could forgive Beau for not sticking up for her when everything had come to a head. Or Melissa for blaming her for the botched barn door, and then Jillian for saying she'd had to fix three of Belle's previous orders but had never said anything.

She also didn't want to try to figure out why she hadn't stood up for herself. It was so much easier to just leave all that in the past, boxed up in a small place in the back of her mind. And going to church made her unpack that box and examine the contents. Relive the situation. Be blamed again. Stay silent.

And she didn't want to do that again. Not today, not the day before she had to go face Jace.

You will have to face him soon, she told herself. *Then what will you do?*

No answer came, and Belle rushed to the TV and turned on the loudest movie she could find. Anything to drown out the worries in her head.

———

The following morning, she took two sips of coffee before pushing it away. She parked at the ranch an hour before her painting crew was slated to arrive. She entered the lodge with such heart palpitations she thought she'd need to see a cardiologist.

Men moved desks, tables, chairs, and bookcases, clearing a wide path around the circumference of the room. She glanced around for Jace but didn't see him.

"Mornin'." A cowboy tipped his white hat at her and continued past to collect a chair still out of place.

Belle marveled at their efficiency, at the way they all worked together, at their quick smiles and bulging muscles. She watched one cowboy wrestle an eight-foot bookcase, singlehandedly moving it from where it had obviously stood for a long time.

"Belle." Landon spotted her and came forward. "How's it looking?"

"Great," she said. "Where will you guys work? We'll be here for a while. I didn't mean you had to move everything away from every wall."

Landon gave her a quick hug. "Boss said we'll have to meet in the break room until you move in there, and we're keeping some stations." He nodded to a couple of desks that barely had room for someone to sit at them. Belle didn't even think she could squeeze herself between the chair and the desk, and no way someone as broad as Jace or Landon could.

"Where is the boss?" she asked.

"Fixin' equipment." He sighed. "It's a never-ending process around here, and Jace is great with a wrench."

Belle wondered what Jace wasn't great with, but she kept that question to herself. "Painters should be here in a little bit. I wanted to talk to Jace first. Do you think he would mind if I went out to see him?"

"Nah." Landon pushed open the door and led her outside. She shoved her gloved hands in her coat pockets at the sudden blast of cold air. "See that rounded, metal building? That's where we keep the tractors and balers and combines. He'll be in there."

"Thanks." She pecked Landon on the cheek and hurried down the steps. Surely the equipment building wasn't heated, but at least the wind wouldn't have the opportunity to steal down the back of her collar.

Her eyes took a few moments to adjust to the dim interior of the building, and she'd been right. It wasn't much warmer in here than outside. She blew on her frigid fingers as she moved down the aisle that separated the massive building into halves.

"Jace?" she called.

"Down here." He poked his head out from between two machines and waved.

She stayed on the path, her heart cartwheeling through her chest. She willed it to settle as she cast her eyes on his bent form. His broad shoulders looked small compared to the jaws of the engine he was working on.

"I wanted to talk about the painting schedule." She had a folder in her purse, but she didn't take it out.

"Go ahead." He didn't look at her, didn't sound happy to see her, didn't seem enthused to entertain her while he worked.

Something about him with grease on his hands and his head under the hood of the tractor spoke to her. She found him more attractive now than ever before. And she had no idea what to do about it.

She cleared her throat, wishing the thoughts about Jace would go as easily. "We'll be a week in the main room of the lodge. It'll take another week to do the offices and the kitchen area. After that, we'll move to the individual cabins." She shuffled through the contents of her purse, her fingers slipping over the file she needed.

Several seconds passed while she tried to get it out, each one increasing her awkwardness. She wasn't sure why she needed it, only that she wanted to have something besides him to look at.

"I put your house first," she said as she found the folder and pulled it out. "It'll take about three days per cabin. We'll move down the row from there, ending with that one way out in the fields."

"That's Tom's." His voice sounded metallic because he still hadn't removed his head from the blasted cavity of the tractor.

"Okay," she said, unsure of what else he wanted. She didn't care who owned which cabin. She just needed him to agree to the schedule. "If each cabin takes three days, that's forty-two days of painting. If we pay them for Saturday, we can have the cabins and the lodge done in nine weeks."

He finally pulled himself to a standing position. "Nine weeks just to paint?"

"You're doing thousands and thousands of square feet." She snapped the folder closed. "And we'll then start on the lodge's floors while the cabins are being painted. Don't worry, *boss*. I aim to have everything done out here at Horseshoe Home in twelve weeks. So we'll paint one week, and then two weeks later, we'll put in carpet, curtains, furnishings, the works. Each cabin will take about a week. The administration lodge will go through three cycles, as we need to do the kitchen area."

His frown deepened the longer she talked, and she finally cut herself off. Did he think she could renovate and remodel fifteen buildings—one of which was four-thousand square feet—in a couple of weeks?

"Boss?" he finally said.

She couldn't see his eyes, as he kept his head ducked while he wiped his hands on a blue rag.

"Right," she said. "You're the boss."

"Not your boss."

"You're absolutely my boss," she said. "You paid me to do a job." She would not let his vulnerability and charm and good looks worm their way under her skin again. He'd made himself clear after their last lunch with his silence and his distance.

Truth was, she probably needed the silence and distance too. And time. Time to figure out what to do after she finished these few jobs she'd contracted. Time to figure out who she was. Time to discover how to forgive.

"Well, my crew will be here in a few minutes. Good day, foreman." She spun on her heel and marched away. The heavier footfalls of Jace came up behind and then beside her, but she didn't look at him.

"I've made you angry," he said.

"Of course you have," she said. "It's what you're best at."

"You're no picnic either."

"You know just how to make a woman feel special." She rolled her eyes and stepped into the bright sunlight, wishing some of its warmth actually made it this far north.

She'd gone a dozen steps when he called, "I'm sorry, Belle. I don't mean to be so good at rubbin' you the wrong way."

She raised her hand to indicate that she'd heard him, but she didn't slow and she didn't look back. Having a conversation with the man made her blood boil. How, exactly, was she thinking they could have a meaningful, long lasting relationship?

The only thing Belle could conclude was that she was delusional. *Not anymore*, she told herself as she ascended the steps and re-entered the lodge. Her crew had obviously just arrived, if the pink tinge in their cheeks said anything.

"Miss Belle," Carlos, the painting team lead, said. "Where should we start?"

———

Jace stayed in the equipment hall longer than necessary. In fact, he could've made his way back with Belle, but her body language screamed angry and frustrated, and he couldn't exactly blame her. At the same time, she owned a phone too. She obviously knew how to use it. Why did the burden to make contact and plan dates always fall on him? Wendy had acted the same way.

Cold fear punctured his lungs, seeped down into his stomach and iced his throat. If Belle was even a hint like Wendy, he couldn't afford to tangle with her.

Problem was, all he thought about was getting closer to her, knowing her better, having her in his life.

"What do you want?" he asked the tractors. None of them responded. But Jace's heart did, loud and clear.

He wanted Belle Edmunds.

CHAPTER 8

*J*ace entered the lodge, expecting to see a crew of men on ladders, with ceilings taped and paint rollers already dipped in the flagstone gray he had chosen. He found Belle directing three men while wearing coveralls, as if she herself would grab a brush and start painting.

As he stared, the men began taping and Belle opened a huge five-gallon bucket of paint. She stirred using an electric blender, and Jace's admiration for her shot to the sky. Watching her work was…strangely appealing. Her strength and knowledge anchored him, and he unconsciously moved toward her.

"Need a hand?"

"Not yours." She didn't look at him as she pulled her long hair back and secured it. "This one's ready, Carlos."

The painter came over and loaded his sprayer while a second man continued taping and the third headed out the front door. Belle took the tray Carlos had poured paint in and began cutting in the gray along the edges.

Jace's mouth went dry watching her work. Sexy, and smart, and hardworking. A triple combination he couldn't fight against. He grabbed a brush and joined her. "I'm sorry," he said under his breath. "I'll be nice, I promise."

Her mouth tightened, but she kept the brush moving.

"You have a phone too," he continued, unable to properly contain his own frustration.

"I didn't think you wanted me to call."

"Why wouldn't I want you to call?" He swiped in time with her. *Swish, swish. Swish, swish.*

"You seemed upset after lunch."

"I...most of that had nothing to do with you."

She paused in her work and looked at him. He was glad he'd asked Landon to get all the boys to move the furniture this morning and then to head out to feed the herd, leaving them virtually alone in the building.

"Then why didn't you call me?"

He shrugged. "I don't know."

She squinted at him. "I think you're telling the truth."

"Thanks for the vote of confidence. You know, you could be nicer too."

Steam practically rose from the top of her head. "I—" Her green eyes sparked with fire, the flame leaping from her to him. In one swift movement—so fast he couldn't move or stop her—she swiped a streak of gray paint across his hand and partway up his arm.

He jerked back and growled. "Oh, it's a good thing you're

wearing coveralls." He lunged at her, but his brush carried hardly any paint. He still managed to muck up both of her hands before she managed to dance away, giggling like getting painted was the best thing that had happened to her in ages.

The door to the lodge closed, and the third painter stood there. He took in Belle and Jace and their paint war before moving to Carlos. They spoke in Spanish, and the guy picked up the last brush and started edging way on the other side from where Belle and Jace stood.

"Guess he doesn't want to join the game." Jace loaded his brush again and went back to work. Belle copied him, but after only a few strokes, she pulled her brush across his clean hand.

"Oops," she said. "Sorry."

"Sorry?" He didn't believe her mocking tone for one second. "You are not sorry."

She giggled and happiness floated through Jace.

He couldn't spend all day doing a job that wasn't his, so after about an hour, he excused himself and headed to his office. His phone rang from the corner of his desk—his mother's ringtone. Jace swiped on the call before considering if he was up to dealing with her.

"Hey, Mom."

"Jace." She sounded upbeat and happy when he answered. "Dinner at your dad's place tonight?"

Jace fell into his chair with a long exhalation. "Who's cookin'?"

"Dad."

"Oh, then, yeah."

"You know, I managed to keep myself alive for almost six decades."

Jace laughed. "By ordering take-out."

His mom laughed too. "All right, fine."

"Should I bring anything?"

"Just yourself."

Apprehension threaded through Jace. "Will Tom be there?"

"I've called him, but he didn't answer."

"He's working, Mom."

"You answered."

"I don't let my cowboys have phones on the job, and they're all out feedin' the herd."

"Where you at?"

"Behind the desk." He sighed as he pulled himself closer to the paperwork waiting for him. "I have reports to read and feed to order. You know, the glamorous side of ranching."

"Well, I won't keep you. Your dad's place around six-thirty."

"See you then." Jace hung up and tried to focus on his work, but his mind kept wandering to the smudge of gray paint still on his knuckle. He'd washed, but that spot had survived. The memory of Belle's giggle and shining eyes wouldn't leave him alone. Maybe she'd like to come to dinner with him—

No, he told himself. He was not taking Belle to a family dinner, even if he felt like the largest fifth wheel on the planet. Mari would be there, and she was good for at least five minutes of conversation, as long as he stuck to horses and dogs.

Six-thirty came, and Jace arrived first to his father's new house up the North canyon, past the waterfalls. He'd bought the land years ago and recently built himself a retirement home. He may have had to quit ranching before he wanted to, but he had a great place to live.

"How's the ranch?" his dad asked.

"Cold." Jace flashed a quick smile toward his dad, who stood at the stove, stirring a huge pot of chili. "How much chili powder did you put in this time?"

"Not enough." His dad harrumphed. "Your mom, she can't stand the burn." He lifted the spoon out and considered the chili. "This is more like stew."

"I'm sure it'll be fantastic." His dad had become a good cook over the years. The first few years after Jace's mom left had been rough for all the Lovell men, Dad included. After that, though, he stepped into the role of both mother and father and learned what was needed. He'd been a good dad.

His dad wasn't one to make idle conversation, but Jace didn't mind. He didn't need the silence stuffed with words, didn't need to know everything about his father's life, and certainly didn't want to share all the details of his. Once his mother arrived, Jace would have to talk, so for the moment, he simply enjoyed the silence.

Until Dad asked, "You seein' someone?"

Jace wrenched his head around so fast, he thought sure he'd kinked his neck. "What? What makes you think that?"

"Heard down at the gas station that you were seen holdin' a woman's hand." He didn't look away from the oven, like the cornbread inside required his undivided attention.

"It was nothing." His words rushed over themselves.

"Nothing? You holdin' your own hand, then?"

"No." Jace's jaw clenched.

"Who was she, then?"

Jace sighed. They'd reached the "then" part of the conversation, and his father would continue to badger him with questions until he got answers.

"She's the ranch's interior designer. I'm sure whoever saw us just misunderstood."

The frown lines between his father's eyes deepened, but he remained quiet. A loud knock sounded on the door, and Jace jumped. In the next moment, his mother walked in, followed by Tom, Rose, and Mari.

Relief roared through Jace—at least if his father didn't mention the hand-holding again. During the commotion of saying hellos, Jace took his turn and retreated to the kitchen, where he brushed melted garlic butter on the cornbread.

"I think it's time you started seein' someone," his dad said in a low voice. So low, Jace could barely hear him. Which meant his mother and brother in the other room certainly couldn't. "She got a name?"

"Belle Edmunds," Jace hissed. "Please don't say anything."

"Gotcha. It's good to see you movin' on."

"I'm not—" Jace started to say, but his dad called, "Time to eat," and Jace couldn't deny that he was moving on.

He *wanted* to move on. He had for a while, but he didn't know how. Maybe holding hands with Belle would help him down that path. He'd felt more alive in the three weeks with her than he had in the past six months. The invisible weight on his shoulders felt lighter as he settled down to dinner next to Mari.

"Hey, there, squirt. Tell me about Silver Creek."

"Pompeii," Mari said as she reached for a square of corn-bread. "He's new. Big horse."

Jace grinned at her. "How many hands?" He caught the grateful look from both Tom and Rose, and for the first time in a long time, he didn't feel like he didn't belong in his own family.

———

Belle was true to her word, and she'd saved a huge part of the commission from Horseshoe Home. She'd also secured the first payment from the Rimrod Lodge, so she could afford to eat out. But she labored in the kitchen, trying to make her pancakes as fluffy and light as the ones she'd eaten at the diner.

"This is impossible," she said after the third failed attempt. "No wonder Jace doesn't like pancakes." The man had been sneaking into her thoughts and dreams a lot lately. In fact, her world had been revolving around him ever since she sauntered into his office.

Someone knocked on the front door, and Belle wiped her hands on her apron as she went to answer it. "Ashley." Belle couldn't help that her voice went up into a squeal on the last syllable of her childhood friend's name. Belle crushed her in a hug. "I haven't seen you in forever."

Ashley laughed and hugged her back with one arm. "Don't smash the bread."

Belle released her instantly. "You brought bread?" Her mouth watered. "How did you know I needed to carbo-load tonight?"

"Rough day?"

"Just long, with a lot of painting." Belle rolled her shoulders. She hadn't minded the work with Jace at her side. As soon as he'd left and gone back to his office, every minute painting felt like a year.

"What are you working on these days?" Ashley stepped into the house and Belle closed the door.

"The Horseshoe Home Ranch." She led Ashley into the kitchen, where the evidence of her failed pancakes lingered. "Never mind this mess. Did you know making fluffy pancakes is impossible?"

"Oh, I know. They must have magic baking soda at the pancake house, because you can't replicate that."

Belle laughed. "It is magical." She accepted the bread Ashley held toward her. "This looks fantastic."

"Don't get your hopes up," she said. "It's just banana bread, and I had my six-year-old help measure the ingredients."

A shadow of sadness slipped through her. She and

Ashley had been best friends in junior high, drifting slightly apart during high school. But Ashley went to college in Missoula while Belle escaped to California. During the years she'd been gone, Ashley had gotten married, started a family, and learned to bake. Things Belle wanted in her life.

"Do you want butter?" She pulled out a serrated knife and a butter dish.

"Of course. What's banana bread without butter?"

Belle smiled as she sliced and buttered. "So, what are you up to these days?"

"Just sitting around, wondering why you've been home for a couple of months and haven't come to see me." The vein of nonchalance in Ashley's tone was clearly forced.

"I'm...sorry, Ashley. It's embarrassing coming home after...." She stuffed her mouth full of banana bread.

Ashley, ever the picture of determined patience, waited until Belle swallowed. "After what?"

"After getting fired." She leveled her gaze at her friend. "I don't think very many people know."

"No one knows."

"What are the rumors?"

"Haven't heard many."

Belle laughed, this time without mirth. "Right. I know this town. No one can go in McCall's without getting some gossip."

Ashley scoffed. "Not McCall's. Please. We've moved past the gas station. Now we get all our juicy stuff at the cupcake shop." She grinned at Belle. "Gentry opened it a few years ago. She's a great baker and everyone loves her creations."

Belle smiled at the memory of their friend. "Good for her. She's just baking cupcakes? Not a full bakery?"

"Just cupcakes." Ashley picked up a piece of bread and took a bite. "Oh, this is fantastic. Jackson will be so excited. He loves to cook with me."

Belle smiled.

"So...word at the shop is that you have yourself a cowboy boyfriend."

Belle choked on her banana bread. "No. That's not true."

"Jace Lovell? He's a cowboy, right? Foreman at the ranch, right?"

Belle fixed Ashley with a glare. "He's not my boyfriend, though. Spread that around."

"Okay." Ashley held up her hands in surrender. "All right."

"Thanks for the bread. Tell your son he did a great job." Belle didn't mean to end the conversation. But she was done with this small town gossip. As Ashley headed for the door, she turned and gave Belle a hug.

"Don't be a stranger," she said. "Come to lunch some-time. Or dinner. Maybe we can drive down to Missoula and go shopping. Remember we used to beg our mothers to let us do that?"

"And they never did." Belle smiled at the memory. "But we went several times anyway." She chuckled. "Oh, if my mother knew...."

Ashley joined her laughter with Belle's. "Have a great night, Belle."

Belle returned to the kitchen and buttered another slice

of banana bread. Since her pancakes hadn't turned out, she needed something to take her mind off the day. Off her tumultuous friendship with Jace. Off the rumors flying around town about her new *cowboy boyfriend*.

If only she could quit thinking about him.

She huffed, turned her back on the last few slices of banana bread, and stalked down the hall to her bedroom. With clean teeth and silky pajamas, a sitcom on loud and the lights turned low, Belle was finally able to get her mind to stop long enough to fall asleep.

CHAPTER 9

Belle worked alongside Carlos and his boys for the entire week. Jace didn't touch a paintbrush again, though he did invite her and the painting crew to lunch each day. She told herself he would've done that whether she was there or not—and she believed it. Which didn't make his invitations special. She ate among thirty men, and she'd never felt more out of her league. By the time she arrived at the house on Friday evening, she needed a pot of chocolate fondue and her fuzzy slippers. She settled for a cup of hot chocolate while she queued up her favorite romantic comedy.

Exhausted, she fell asleep minutes after finishing her hot chocolate, but the chirp-chirp of her phone woke her minutes later. Her heart raced and her eyes flew open. It took a few seconds for her to place the sound and reach for her phone.

Want to sit by me at church? Jace had texted.

She marveled at his stamina. He worked the way she had this week every week, all day, every day.

I didn't see you last week. Landon said you were sick. How are you feeling this week?

Tired, she texted. *I was actually asleep.*

Oh, sorry. I'll leave you to your nap.

Belle's spirits, which had been rising, sank. Had she just admitted that her Friday night consisted of her dozing off? How pathetic did that make her?

She slumped back against her pillows. Her aching muscles and over-tired mind didn't care what she'd just said. She managed to send one last text before she snuggled back into her blankets.

Yes, I'll sit by you at church.

The time for church came quicker than Belle expected. She blinked and Saturday was gone, took a breath and found herself walking into the chapel for services, her gaze sweeping from left to right as she searched for Jace.

She didn't have to look far. He stood just inside the doors, obviously waiting for her. "Mornin', sunshine."

She warmed from the inside out with the simple sound of his voice. "Morning, boss."

His eyes hardened into black marbles. "Don't."

"Relax, Jace. I was joking."

He visibly softened from the set of his shoulders to the clenching in his jaw. He offered her his arm and she took it. Every eye in the place seemed fixed on them as they strolled down the aisle to a bench near the front. She normally didn't put herself on such display, but her brother had saved a space on the end of the bench for Jace.

Shock waves traveled down her back. She hadn't discussed her attraction to Jace with Landon, with anyone. Jace obviously hadn't either, because as he ushered her onto the bench so she could sit next to her brother, Landon did a double take.

"Belle." He half-stood, his gaze moving between her and Jace. Landon sat again and gave Belle an awkward side-hug. "You here with him?"

"No," she said quickly. "We were just walking in together."

Landon gave a curt nod and turned back to the front of the chapel. Jace pressed in closer than necessary, his leg nearly flush against hers. She sucked in a breath when his hand found hers and settled their joined fingers on his leg.

"This okay?" he murmured. "Or did you want to keep lyin' to Landon about meetin' me on the way in?"

She turned to look at him, and found him close. So close. Too close. Close enough to kiss if she wanted to. And oh, she wanted that kiss. She licked her lips as she tried to settle her pulse.

"I—I didn't know what to say," she whispered. "Do you think he'll be upset?"

"Why would he be upset?"

"Well, I—I'm his little sister."

"Yeah, and we're adults." Jace's warm breath cascaded over her shoulder, causing her nerves to riot and her desire for him to skyrocket. "But you're right. I should probably talk to him before we start datin'." He leaned down, his mouth almost touching her earlobe. She didn't dare breath, couldn't even move.

"That is, if you want to admit you like me and didn't just find me lurking in the lobby."

The pastor got up, but Belle whispered, "Fine, I get it. You're mad I didn't—"

"Shh." Jace shushed her—actually *shushed* her—at the same time he put a healthy foot of distance between them and removed his hand from hers. He cast her a sour glance when she looked at him for an explanation.

She glared back. Belle expected him to look away once the opening song started. Then she'd win. But he didn't. Just stared at her with that dark, dangerous glint in his eye that did more to excite her than it did to scare her.

She scooted closer. "I'm not afraid of you."

"Yes, you are."

"No, I'm not."

"You're afraid to be seen with me."

"No, I'm not."

"You're afraid to admit you like me. You're—"

"Shh." The elderly man in front of them turned around and frowned. Jace lifted his hand in a silent apology, then cast Belle a look filled with challenge, hurt, and fear. The older gentleman turned around, Belle faced the pastor, and Jace got up and left.

———

Jace couldn't sit next to Belle for one more second. She obviously didn't understand how hurtful it was to hear her tell Landon that she wasn't there with him. Jace felt like someone had jammed a knife into his gut. His cowboy boots clunked the whole way down the aisle, an endless retreat. He couldn't fathom what his face looked like, but concerned eyes and curious glances landed on him as he approached then passed. He hated breaking down in front of other people, but at the same time, he couldn't keep up his strong man act much longer.

He managed to make it out of the chapel before he wheezed. He didn't stop there, but hurried to his truck and secured himself inside before starting the ignition.

Then he just drove.

He steered his truck alongside the river, all the way up to the horseshoe waterfalls. He'd spent a lot of time fishing in this river and splashing in the pool at the bottom of the falls. Wide and short, they created a deafening noise he'd always loved.

He pulled into the parking lot and rolled down the window. Even though February had just begun and the weather still hovered below zero, the swift-moving water kept the falls liquid, though not as much water dropped over the twelve foot ledge.

After dinner with his family, Jace had decided to take a chance. He'd been encouraged by Belle's response about sitting with him at church, and while he may not have thought through sitting by Landon, he certainly hadn't expected Belle to deny being with him.

His nose tingled in the cold, and he rolled up his window. Every muscle in his body felt stretched too tight, and he hated it. Hated feeling so disposable. Hated feeling so weak.

He backed out and turned toward town. He drove past the church and into the heart of Gold Valley. Houses surrounded the city center, which boasted busy parks in the summer, the best Italian food at locally-owned Migliano's, and a long row of shops on both sides of the street. Jace had loved buying penny candy at the corner store, ducking into the bookshop on hot summer afternoons, and racing Tom back to the river before their dad discovered they'd left their poles unattended.

He drove across the railroad tracks, turning when he felt like it. He hadn't spent much time in town beyond going to school and the occasional day-trip to fish and wander Main Street. Ranching was an around-the-clock job, and his father had expected his sons to help.

Jace returned to the main road, and headed toward Silver Creek. Tom had said nothing but good things about the therapeutic riding program there, even suggesting that perhaps Jace could benefit from the equine therapy. For ten seconds, Jace considered pulling in and finding someone to ask about the program. In the end, he continued up the mountain, where an exclusive cabin community could only be accessed through a gate equipped with a code. A code he didn't have.

He turned around and retraced his path, once again bypassing the church in favor of heading up the canyon and back to the ranch. Before Tom had returned to Montana, Jace hadn't been much of a church-goer. But he'd gone along with his brother and he'd found value in the messages he heard. He felt something once he started going to church, once he started paying attention to others more than himself, once he felt God's love for him.

After Wendy had left, Jace had craved the peace attending church had brought him. Now, though, he needed more.

He needed answers.

He needed closure.

He needed someone more than God to love him.

His truck bounced over the ruts in the road leading to the ranch, jarring Jace out of his thoughts. Though true, they only fueled his frustration. He didn't know how to achieve closure, or how to make someone love him enough to stick around. Heck, he'd take someone liking him enough to admit it to their brother.

He skidded to a stop when he realized a red sedan sat in front of his house—where he usually parked. As his anger amped up, Belle unfolded herself from the driver's seat. She cocked her hip and folded her arms as if to say, "Well, it's about time you showed up."

Jace got out of his truck and mimicked her body language. "What are you doin' here?"

"I wanted to talk to you, but you apparently didn't come straight home."

He shrugged. "Drove around a bit. Cleared my head."

"Oh, is that all it takes?" Her honeyed voice dripped with poison. "You thinking more clearly now?"

"I've been thinking clearly all along, sunshine."

She snorted. "Obviously not."

"You *are* afraid to be seen with me. You can't admit you like me. Not even to your own brother. Not even to yourself."

She marched toward him, her fingers balled in fists. For a moment, he thought she'd barrel right into him, and he braced himself. But she stopped with only eight inches to spare. "I like you," she said through clenched teeth. "Happy now?"

"I like you, too," he shot back. "I'm interested in getting to know you better, if you want that too."

"I do."

"Great."

"Fine."

Jace wasn't sure if he should haul her into his arms and kiss her or steer clear of those fists. Judging from the fire in her eyes, she could've gone either way. "You want to come in and have some coffee?" he asked. "It's mighty cold out here."

"What kind of coffee do you have?"

"Oh, brother," he muttered. "If it's not up to your standards, you're welcome to leave." He stepped past her, wondering why he was so drawn to a woman he could barely tolerate.

"I didn't say it wouldn't be up to my standards," she said

as she moved with him. "I don't even have standards for coffee. You can't keep putting words in my mouth."

He paused with his foot on the bottom step. "You're right." The fight left his body. "I'm sorry."

She stepped up onto the first stair so their eyes were level. "You need to get it into your head that I'm not your ex."

"What? That has nothing—"

"She has everything to do with why you're all worked up over simple things."

"You told Landon you weren't there with me." His voice rose, and he swallowed to keep it from getting louder. "That —how do you think that made me feel? How would you like it if Tom asked me if we came together and I said no?"

"We didn't come together."

"We planned to meet and sit together." He shook his head. He couldn't make her understand. As he continued up the stairs he said, "I don't think you're Wendy. She has nothing to do with you rejecting me while I sat a foot away. That was all you, Belle."

CHAPTER 10

*B*elle's heart beat furiously in her chest, drumming up into her ears and causing tears to form in her eyes. She *had* rejected him. Right in front of him, she'd rejected him. She watched him disappear into his house, the screen door slamming closed behind him. He didn't close the solid wood door, though, and she squared her shoulders and marched up the stairs after him.

Be nice, she told herself for the hundredth time. She'd coached herself to *be nice* on the entire drive here. As she waited nearly an hour for him to show up. But something about him made her blurt whatever came into her mind.

She entered the house and softly pushed the door closed behind her. Jace stood in the kitchen, his back to her.

"Jace," she said. "I'm really sorry."

He swiveled toward her, his face shadowed by his hat. But his body language screamed tense and guarded.

"You're right." She slipped through the living room and stood chest-to-chest with him. "I didn't think. And I'm sorry. I do like you, and I don't care who sees us." Fear flowed through her, but she didn't blink, didn't look away.

"I like you, too, sunshine." One hand came up to cradle her cheek while the other swept around her waist. He leaned down and inhaled her hair before pressing his lips to her forehead. Belle leaned into his touch, inhaling his warm, spicy scent and feeling safe in his arms. She imagined, just for a moment, of this being her reality, of going to church with him every week, coming home with him, sharing stories over coffee, and kissing to make-up every time they disagreed.

Happiness and peace poured through her. "Sorry," she murmured again.

"Apology accepted." He cleared his throat and fell back a step. "So I have coffee, tea, or hot chocolate. Pick your poison."

She wondered if he was on the menu, and how dangerous to her health he would be, but she kept that thought to herself—for once—and pointed to the coffee.

With the coffee brewed and doctored up the way she liked it, she moved into his living room and curled into his couch. He sat next to her, far enough to be comfortable and close enough to convey he wanted to get closer.

"Tell me what you did in Sacramento." His tone didn't demand, didn't suspect, only asked. Politely too.

"Same thing I'm doing here. Interior design."

He nodded as he sipped his coffee. "Mm, this is good."

"You did a good job," she agreed.

"You added more hazelnut cream than coffee," he said.

She took a sip of the hazelnut concoction—with a hint of coffee in the background. "It's so good. I mean, have you had hazelnut cream?"

"Obviously," he said. "As this is my house, and you just drained the last of my supply."

Guilt tripped through her and she lowered her mug. "You said I could drink it."

He chuckled as he leaned forward and placed his coffee on the table. When he sat back, his arm came around her shoulders, tucking her securely against his side. "You can. I'm glad you like it." He took a deep breath, and Belle snuggled an inch closer. She felt adored, like he couldn't get enough of her.

"Sometimes I'd go surfing," she said. "But it was a long drive. So we really just stuck to the riverfronts. We'd picnic or rent some jet skis. That kind of thing."

"You like surfing?"

She drained the rest of her coffee. "Not really."

"Who's 'we'?" he asked.

Her muscles spasmed, and she couldn't hide the fact from Jace. Next to her, his lean body tensed, creating a hard wall of muscle. "Uh—I'd go surfing with my boyfriend. We both loved the ocean." She wanted to look into his eyes when she mentioned a boyfriend, but she couldn't tip her head back far enough without being obvious.

"You and this boyfriend, it's still a thing?"

"Of course not." She sat up and twisted toward him. "You think I'd be here if it was?"

His expression stormed, but he relaxed. "Sorry. Of course you wouldn't. So you broke up?"

Everything Belle wished could be erased from her life came roaring back. "Yes, we broke up after he didn't back me up on one of my projects. He's still there." She chewed her bottom lip, her mind about as far from Gold Valley as it could get. "He's one of the people I need to forgive."

"Ah." Jace reached for her and gently pulled her back to his side. "What happened on the project?" His breath tickled her ear, and she imagined his lips to be so close, not close enough. Nerves ran down her arms, making her shiver.

"You cold? I can light a fire."

Nothing could be more romantic, and building a fire would take him at least a few minutes. "Sure, a fire sounds great."

He left her on the couch while he went to the wood closet off the back porch. Belle worried through telling him what had happened in California. Would he judge her? Think her incompetent? Wish he hadn't hired her for the huge renovation at Horseshoe Home?

Trust him.

The words resonated in her mind until Belle's anxiety faded. He returned and started stacking the wood in a pattern she didn't understand. But when he crinkled newspaper, stuffed it in the cracks, and held a lighter to it, the wood caught almost immediately.

He turned back to her and clapped his hands together.

She took a deep breath. "I was fired in Sacramento."

He flinched, but quickly regained his stoic expression. "That's too bad." He stepped into her and gathered her into a warm embrace. She pressed her cheek against his chest and relished the feeling of safety within the circle of his arms.

"But I'm kinda glad," he whispered. "Because now you're here."

She'd never considered what doors would open from losing her job in Sacramento. But now, with the heat of the fire licking her face and the warmth from Jace permeating her senses, Belle thanked the Lord for putting her on the path she needed to be on, even when she didn't know where that path would lead and she had to experience some hard things to find it.

———

Jace thought he could hold Belle forever. She fit against him, fit into his life. Easier than he thought possible. Wendy always seemed to buck against who Jace was—he'd just never known it until she left. He realized now that she never fit on the ranch, that she wouldn't have been happy here. He wasn't sure Belle would either, but she'd at least try.

"So, your turn," Belle said as she settled back onto the couch. "Tell me something about your life here."

He gestured to his house, the ranch beyond it. "This is my life. It's pretty mundane."

A crinkle appeared between her eyebrows. There, then gone in a flash. "There has to be more."

"Sorry to disappoint you." He sat next to her but didn't reach to touch her. "I've always wanted to see the ocean."

"You've never even seen it?"

"Not in real life."

"But you're like, thirty years old."

He cocked one eyebrow at her. "What does that have to do with anything? And I'm thirty-two, for the official record."

"Your parents never took you on vacation?"

"My dad ran this place for thirty years," Jace said. "And my mom skipped out on us when we were young, remember?" He suddenly felt so inadequate to be Belle's boyfriend. She'd experienced things beyond Gold Valley, and well, he hadn't. Horseshoe Home was all he knew, and until this very moment, it had been enough.

"Maybe we could go," he suggested. "Me and you."

She blinked, reached for her coffee cup, and frowned into it when she found it empty. "Sure. But not northern California. We should go to San Diego."

"Sure." He threaded his fingers through hers. "After the reno."

"After the reno," she echoed, her voice distant. He switched on the TV, having had enough conversation to last a week, and Belle dozed against his chest for the better part of two hours. Jace sank into slumber too, the most content he'd been since his botched wedding day months ago.

The next morning, he shouldn't have been surprised to

find Landon lounging in his office, but the sight of the size twelve cowboy boots propped on his desk did annoy him. "Can I help you with something?" Jace moved behind the desk and leaned his fists into it as he tilted forward.

Landon glared at him. "So you're dating my sister."

"She's twenty-nine-years-old," Jace said. "She can make her own decisions."

Landon thought about that, even nodded to acknowledge its truth. "I don't get it. You two never get along."

"We get along fine." The tension left Jace's body, and he sank into the chair opposite Landon. "She's...she makes me feel like living again." He glanced over Landon's shoulder, not really looking at anything. "I haven't felt like that in a long time. It's...nice."

Landon's frosty exterior melted. "With what you've been through the past year, I guess I can't blame you." He stood and stared down at Jace. "Be careful, boss. Belle is a firecracker."

"I'm not going to hurt her."

"It's not her I'm worried about." Landon tipped his hat and walked out, leaving Jace's heartbeat pulsing in the back of his throat. It was good to know he and Landon were watching out for each other. Nice to know he had friends he could trust, could count on. Friends who understood and cared about him.

Thank you, he prayed. He'd needed to know he had more than God watching out for him. And now he knew he had Landon in his corner, even if things went south with Belle.

He worked through the day, the week, and the weekend.

He took a shift every couple of months to give his cowboys a day off. That Sunday, he and Tom took the day to feed the herd before they retired to Tom's cabin. Rose bustled around as she made cookies, and Mari stayed downstairs where another TV kept her occupied.

"Thanks for helping," Jace said. "Sorry you had to miss church."

"It's once every few months." Tom yawned and laid his head against the back of the couch. "But feedin' the herd by yourself is tiring."

"Sure is."

Companionable silence ensued, and Jace enjoyed spending time with his brother, a luxury he'd missed for years while Tom worked in Texas. "I'm seeing Belle Edmunds," he finally said.

That got Tom to shoot straight up, his eyes open wide as he searched Jace's face. "You are?"

A slow smile spread across Jace's face. "It's a new development."

"I saw you stomp out of church last week. She followed a few minutes later. Didn't want to say anything about it." He ran his hand over his unshaven face. "Wow, Belle Edmunds."

"She's a bit out of my league, isn't she?"

"That's not what I meant." Tom peered at his brother. "You deserve a good woman in your life, Jace. Is she that?"

Jace's sarcasm and humor went out the window. "I think so. I'm just gettin' to know her. But she goes to church, and she works hard, and she's kind. Well, at least to other people."

Tom quirked half a smile. "You two never did get along."

Trepidation pulled through Jace. "You're the second person to say that this week. We get along fine." But maybe they didn't. "She just...riles me up."

"And you like that." Tom wasn't asking, but he watched Jace closely, which made Jace pause to find the right answer.

"It was always just playful banter. We have a lot in common, actually. She's easy to talk to, and she makes me feel...." He cleared his throat, because he'd never told Tom how he felt after Wendy left. He suspected his brother knew —he'd suggested the equine therapy, after all—but Jace had never said it. "She makes me feel like I have something worth livin' for."

"Jace." The fear and disappointment on Tom's face didn't settle Jace's nerves.

"It's just that, you know, after Wendy left, I wondered if my life had a purpose. So I could run Horseshoe Home for thirty years by myself, break my hip, and move into a newer, nicer version of a bachelor pad across the canyon?" Jace ducked his head and studied his hands. "I don't want that life. I mean, I love the ranch. Love Montana. Don't feel the itch to move or anything. But I...I don't want to live Dad's life. He's lonely, Tom, and I don't want to be alone forever."

Jace's voice stuck in his throat, so he stopped talking. He'd never expressed his loneliness so fully before. He wasn't even sure he'd felt it so keenly before now.

"I understand," Tom said.

"Thanks." Jace looked up and gave his brother a grateful

smile. "And there's a lot of things I don't know about Belle." Like where she was going to live once her parents returned. He hoped she'd stay in Gold Valley, but they still needed to discuss that particular point. "This is a brand new thing."

"What's brand new?" Rose appeared with a plate of warm cookies. Tom took one and indicated that Jace should tell her if he wanted.

He took a cookie and said, "Thanks, Rose. I just started dating Belle Edmunds."

Rose gasped and set the plate of cookies on the table. "That's so great, Jace. Congratulations."

"They're not engaged," Tom muttered. "Don't make a big deal out of this."

Jace could tell Rose wanted to make a big deal out of it, and he realized how secluded, how moody, how detached he'd become. "Thanks, Rose," he said again. "It is kind of a big deal, isn't it?"

She patted his hand and squeezed his fingers. "I'm so happy for you. I know what it's like to try to move on after a disastrous relationship." She glanced at Tom, who stared at her with a blank expression. "Some people don't get it, because they haven't been there. If you need someone to talk to, I'm right here." She stood and sniffed, and Jace once again had a flash of realization that the people surrounding him cared about him, loved him, and wanted him to be happy.

"You take the time you need, too," she said. "Okay? Promise me you'll take the time you need to get to the right place."

Jace volleyed his gaze from Tom to Rose and back. His brother had moved up here alone, worked and lived here by himself before Rose showed up. She'd been figuring things out, learning how to get to the right place.

"I will," he promised her—and himself.

CHAPTER 11

*B*elle didn't join Carlos and his crew as they moved onto painting the cowboy cabins. Number one, she didn't want to get too up-close and personal with Jace's belongings. Their relationship was too new for that, and she thought he'd appreciate being able to keep his own space for now. Number two, she had a lot of work to get done for the Rimrod Lodge, as well as a meeting with the director of Flathead Lake.

She called Ashley one morning in late February, hoping her friend would be awake. "How do you feel about a day-trip to Flathead Lake?" she asked when Ashley answered. "You and Jackson."

"Flathead Lake?"

"I have a meeting out there with their director for a project, and I don't want to make the drive alone. You guys could go ice fishing, or skating, or I looked up their junior ranger program, and it's mostly indoors this time of year. We could get lunch, or—"

"You had me at ice skating." Ashley laughed. "What time do we need to be ready?"

"About nine," Belle said, a smile skimming her lips. "Thanks, Ash. I'm buying today, too. I hear there's a great café out on Wild Horse Island. We'd have to take a boat, but the website says it's heated. My meeting's at one-thirty. Then we'll come home."

"We'll be ready," Ashley said, and Belle hung up. Overjoyed she didn't have to make the long drive alone, she also wanted to talk about Jace and work through some of her confusing feelings. Over the past couple of weeks, if she was out working at the ranch, he invited her to stay for dinner. The man could cook, too, and every time she thought about why he knew his way around the kitchen, sadness permeated her thoughts.

Then she'd spiral down a dark hole that ended with his fiancé standing him up on their wedding day. She couldn't abandon him the same way. She didn't want to be that woman, so she'd backed way off. They hadn't cuddled on the couch again, and he hadn't once tried to kiss her goodbye. She had a feeling he was also testing the waters before diving in too deep. He didn't want to get hurt again. She certainly didn't want to be the one to hurt him.

And so they'd come to a bit of a crossroads, neither one willing to take the next step. She dreamed, fantasized, and thought constantly about kissing him before leaving the ranch, but wanted to give him the time he needed to get there by himself.

She packed up her proposal and portfolio, though Vic should already have a copy of both. She phoned into the office to tell Calvin she'd be going to Flathead Lake that day. With nothing left to do, she typed out a quick text to Jace. *Going to see about a new account today. Wish me luck!*

Belle stared at the message, trying to decide if she could add more to it. Maybe an emoji heart or something. In the end, she pressed send and stuffed her phone in her purse. If Jace was out on the ranch, he wouldn't answer right away. With it being the beginning of the week, she suspected it would be lunchtime before he looked at his phone. He seemed to do paperwork and office things on Thursdays and Fridays.

Warmed by the realization that she knew his schedule, Belle set out to pick up her friend. Only a few miles into the drive, Ashley had Jackson set up with a tablet, a movie, and a pair of headphones.

"So, tell me about your cowboy boyfriend." She practically glowed with repressed glee. "He is your boyfriend now, right?"

Belle couldn't help the grin that sprang to her face. "Right."

Ashley squealed. "I love being right."

"Well, we decided after our first conversation. So I didn't lie to you last time." She glanced at Ashley and back to the lonely two-lane highway.

"Oh, I know. I've never dated a cowboy. Is he—? Tell me everything."

"Isn't every man here a cowboy?"

Ashley laughed. "It seems that way, but no. Carter works in construction. He's terribly handy, which I enjoy. He built our house from the ground up."

"Wow." Belle did enjoy a man who was good with his hands, and she'd seen Jace's painting and mechanic skills. Her skin prickled with the thought of his hands touching her. She sighed. "It's going slow, which is fine. I'm just...I need some advice."

Ashley crossed her legs. "Well, you've come to the right person. What's going on?"

"You know his fiancé left him at the altar, right?"

"Yes. So sad." Ashley shook her head. "He hasn't dated since."

"I understand why."

"So does he not act interested?"

"He does—to an extent. He's pushy and stubborn at the same time. He wants me to admit how I feel, but we haven't kissed or anything."

Ashley sighed. "Oh, that's a shame. I imagine a man like Jace being quite the kisser."

"Ashley!" Belle laughed, but it sounded awkward and forced.

"Sorry, sorry." Ashley grinned. "You want to kiss him, right?"

"Of course. But I think he's trying to figure out if I'm worth his time." As she spoke, she realized the truth of her words. "In fact, that's exactly what he's doing: judging me worthy enough to get involved with. If I fail, he'll break things off. He doesn't want to get abandoned again." She took a deep breath and pressed harder on the accelerator. "And I don't blame him. I don't. I just...do you think I can speed him up a little?"

Ashley remained quiet for a few minutes, and when she spoke, her voice carried an edge of gravity. "Here's the thing, Belle. This only ends one of two ways for a man in Jace's position. With a wedding—and one that doesn't have a year-long engagement, by the way—or a break-up in the next few weeks. I don't see him going all the way just to get hurt again."

"I know. You're right."

"So you have to know that, and then decide: Is that how this ends for you too? Are you ready to get married in the next, say, six months? *Married*, Belle. Not engaged."

Belle's stomach seemed to want to abandon her body. It twisted and turned. "I don't even live here. Not really. When my parents come back—I mean, I'm almost thirty years old. I'm not going to live with them."

"And a man as smart as Jace knows that. So every day you continue to live in your parent's house is a day he can't take a chance with you." Ashley reached over and patted her leg. "You have money, right? Can you get a place of your own? Oooh, I know! Carter's working on a new development on the northern edge of town. Right after the falls. You been up there?"

Belle shook her head, unsure if she actually wanted to

buy something. If this relationship only ended in marriage for Jace, wouldn't she live with him on the ranch? Her mind spun, and she tightened her grip on the steering wheel so she didn't lose control. She couldn't believe she was considering marriage. Marriage to a man she hadn't even kissed yet.

She and Beau had dated for two years, and the M-word had never even surfaced. But deep down, Belle knew Ashley was right. Jace wouldn't wait. If he discovered he loved her, he'd want to get married straightaway. The man made decisions and acted on them—a quality she admired.

"I think I'd rather rent," she said.

"One of my friends is a real estate agent. I'll give you her number." Ashley began scrolling on her phone. "I'm so excited for you, Belle. Jace is a great man. Strong and stable and sensitive."

Belle tuned her out as she focused on the twisty road. Jace *was* a great man. He *was* strong, and stable, and sensitive. A surge of uneasiness swept over her. "What if I do all this—get somewhere to live, and kiss him, and he doesn't think I'm worth his time?"

"Well, that would be impossible. Have you seen yourself? You're gorgeous. You're successful. You're kind. Why wouldn't he want to be with you?"

Belle's lips pressed together as she thought about how *un*successful she was, even if it appeared to be the opposite to someone on the outside. "He rubs me the wrong way sometimes."

Ashley laughed—a full-on belly laugh. "Oh, honey,

Carter rubs me the wrong way sometimes too. Every time he turns the TV on right when its time to go to bed." She made a face. "You work through those things when you love someone."

"I'm not in love with him," Belle murmured.

"Not yet," Ashley said. "Give it some time. And I texted you Paulie's number. She'll find you somewhere to live lickety split."

Relief coated Belle's words when she said, "Thanks, Ash. You're the best."

———

It was the first day of spring—and the temperatures were actually melting some of the winter snow—when Jace jerked in surprise at the message on his phone.

From Belle: *I need your help to move into my new place this weekend. You free?*

He pressed call and waited impatiently while the line rang. When she answered, he said, "You're moving?"

"That's right. I got a house in town."

"Your own house?"

"I'm renting for now," she said, her voice somewhat aloof, though that could've been his imagination. He'd been circling the idea of kissing her, of taking their relationship to the next level, but he hadn't been able to do it. They'd spent a lot of time together over the past six weeks; he knew most of her dislikes, had asked about her beliefs, gotten answers for almost everything he needed to know. But he'd never asked her what her plans were once her parents returned.

Now he didn't need to.

Or maybe he did. "You're planning to stay in Gold Valley for a while?"

"Why do you sound so surprised?" She giggled. "I have a job here, Jace. I have four clients now, and I'm busy. I like it here, well, I will once all this snow melts. And I happen to have a very handsome boyfriend I want to keep."

"When can I see you?" he asked, his grip tightening on his phone. She'd made herself a permanent fixture in Gold Valley. It had been the last thing Jace needed before he advanced things with her. He'd kept his promise to himself —and to Rose—by going slow, taking the time he needed to work through his frustrations and feelings. He still hadn't forgiven Wendy, but he reasoned that she had nothing to do with Belle.

He realized she was still talking, and he focused on the sexy sound of her voice. "...so maybe Thursday? Does that work?"

"That's days away," he complained.

She laughed. "Call me later, cowboy. We can talk while I sort through paint chips."

"Or I can come help you," he suggested.

"Oh, I don't think that would be wise. I wouldn't actually get any work done with you here."

"Sure you would." Confusion raced through him. "I've been over and let you work before. I even fell asleep that one time, remember?"

"I don't think you have sleeping on your mind right now." Her playful tone indicated that she knew he'd been holding back—and that she knew why. Joy lifted his spirits. She knew him, and she knew what he needed, and she'd done what he'd needed so she could be with him.

"Fine," he sighed. "Thursday."

"Perfect. I'll see you here for dinner."

"You cookin'?"

"I'll order your favorite." She hung up before he could question her. And she was right. He wouldn't be able to wait for dinner before thoroughly kissing her. He wanted to abandon his chores on the ranch and go right now. But with spring right around the corner, he had fields to prepare for planting and paddocks to repair so they could move the herd off of hay and into the pastures. Not to mention that branding season was only two months off and none of their equipment was anywhere near ready.

The good news was that the renovation on the ranch was nearing completion. The lodge had gotten a facelift with the gray paint and dark carpet. The bookshelves, tables, and chairs had all been painted eggshell, and everything looked shiny and new. Even Jace enjoyed his new office, with its black and white chevron curtains. He hadn't known what a chevron was, but as he faced the design, he smiled. Belle left her mark everywhere, and he liked her presence at the ranch even when she wasn't there.

He fantasized about kissing her and didn't notice when Rob knocked or came in. "Jace, we need you in our meeting."

Jace yanked himself out of his daydreams. "Sure thing, boss." He followed Rob down the hall to his office, his mind like a sieve. He needed to figure out how to focus, but all he could hear was "I got a house in town."

Thursday night seemed to take forever to come. At the same time, the hours at the ranch passed in a rush. With so much keeping him busy, Jace could only spare a few minutes each night before he fell asleep to think about Belle.

He arrived at Belle's at the same time a spring storm decided to drop buckets of water. He raced through the rain to her front porch and found her waving him inside.

"Hey." He took off his dripping wet hat and shook the water from it.

"Wow."

He glanced up at the awe in her voice. She floated toward him, her hands reaching up to stroke through his hair. He closed his eyes and enjoyed the magical touch of this woman.

"I've never seen your hair," she whispered. Already on her tiptoes, she pressed against him. "It's so good to see you." She fiddled with his hair on the nape of his neck, and Jace put his hands on the small of her back to hold her close.

"I thought Thursday would never come." He brushed his lips against her forehead, down one cheek. She tilted her head to lean into his touch. "Belle, I'm dyin' to kiss you." His voice sounded strangled and husky.

Hers sounded flirty and in complete control when she said, "What are you waitin' for, then?"

He dropped his gaze to her mouth; he didn't wait

another moment. He touched his lips to hers, expecting an explosion—and getting one. She was a firecracker and Jace wanted to experience every pop, spark, and snap.

She tasted like chocolate and mint, and she kissed him back with the same passion running through his veins. He'd never been kissed like that, and he drew her closer and deepened their connection.

CHAPTER 12

Kissing Jace could only be described as life-changing. Everything Belle had dreamt about came true—right down to the heat coiling through her and the intense pressure of his hands on her back.

"I've missed you," he whispered against her lips. He kissed her again, and Belle let herself fall, fall, fall. She adored him, and she wanted him to know it. She tried to pour everything she felt into her kiss, and by the time they parted, her lips felt bruised and swollen. He leaned his forehead against hers, his breathing ragged and quick.

A moment later, a deep chuckle emanated from his chest. "Don't know why I waited so long to do that."

"You 'bout killed me too," she said.

"Thank you." He touched his lips to hers for a quick, chaste kiss. "Thank you for giving me time."

Her chest squeezed, but she smiled and caught hold of

the bravery she needed to tell him what she'd been practicing. "Jace, I'm not planning on hurting you again."

"I know." He stroked his hands up and down her back, his mouth positioned just above her ear.

"So I know this has to end well—for both of us. If you need more time—at any time—or I do, we should give each other that."

"Of course."

"So it's a deal?" She leaned back, because she couldn't actually step away what with the way he held onto her so tightly.

His eyes shone with adoration; deep dark pools of desire. "Sure, Belle. It's a deal."

She sighed against his chest and held on, memorizing this moment so she could recall it when she needed something perfect to get her through a tough time. After several minutes, she cleared her throat. "So I did actually order pizza."

He relinquished his vice-grip on her body, but slid his hand down to hers. "What kind?"

"If it doesn't meet your standards, you're welcome to leave."

He froze and stared at her for one, two, three heartbeats before his booming laugh filled her house. "Wow, I can't believe I said that to you."

She smiled. "I deserved it at the time." She flipped open the pizza box. "Meat lovers."

He gazed at her, and Belle stared back. "You really do know me."

"I really do. Which is why I need you here on Saturday morning at eight to get my stuff moved." She pushed him playfully. "I know you'll be up at the crack of dawn, so don't pretend like eight is early." She pointed to the paper plates so he'd get something to eat.

"Is Landon comin' to help?"

"Yep, and my friend's husband, Carter. Ashley will help me get this place cleaned and closed up for the summer. We're putting sheets on the furniture and stuff." She took a slice of pizza and pulled a bagged salad out of the fridge while he glanced around.

"It shouldn't take too long," he said. "I assume most of this stuff stays here."

"I have a storage unit."

He groaned, and she laughed. "Oh, brother. A big, strong cowboy like you can't handle a storage unit?"

"What you got in there?"

"Antique furniture." She grinned at the horrified look on his face. "And after you get me all set up in my new place, you can take me to lunch."

He cracked the top on a can of soda as he sat on her couch. "I don't see how I'm benefitting from any of this."

She sat next to him and set her plate on the table. She carefully took his and placed it next to hers. Then she pressed into him and kissed him like she'd never kissed a man before. She liked the taste of him in her mouth, liked the way he held her carefully like he could break her with his bare hands.

"All right," he whispered into her mouth. "I get it. Can I kiss you like this in your new place?"

"Anywhere you want, cowboy."

He growled—a sexy, deep sound that ignited a fire in Belle's belly—and kissed her again.

Jace shook Carter North's hand. He knew the carpenter from odd jobs around the ranch. Carter had even shown Jace the best way to rung a fence so the snows wouldn't deteriorate the line. Jace had taught all his cowboys, and the ranch's fences stayed in good repair much longer.

On Thursday, when Jace had been at Belle's, he hadn't seen a single box. But when she opened the door on Saturday morning, the foyer held about a dozen taped and labeled boxes. He appreciated her organization and wanted to kiss her hello. But with Carter there and Carlos backing up the moving truck, Jace kept his hands to himself.

"Thanks for coming." Belle beamed at him, a glint in her eye that said she wanted to kiss him too. "We're just loading up here before heading over to the storage unit. Then we'll go to my new place."

"This is it?" Jace swept the boxes.

"I have a few more things in the garage. We should start there; that's where the big stuff is."

Carter obediently moved through the living room and kitchen to the garage exit. Jace heard the rumble of the door as it opened and swooped into Belle's personal space.

"Mornin'." He gathered her close, pressing his lips to hers in that kiss he wanted. When she didn't react as enthusiastically as she had on Thursday, he asked, "You okay?"

"Just nervous," she whispered against his chest. She held him tighter than normal, and Jace wanted to erase all of her worries, all of her fears.

"Why?" he asked.

"New place." She shrugged one shoulder as she stepped back a couple of inches. "Feels...grown-up."

He scanned her face, trying to find the real problem, but he couldn't. "You like your new place?"

"Yeah, I looked at about a half-dozen houses. This one's nice."

"Worried about the neighborhood?" Gold Valley didn't have a high crime rate, but some of the neighborhoods had been around for decades and were a little run-down.

She removed herself from his embrace completely and went into the kitchen, rubbing her arms as if cold. "The neighborhood's fine."

"Then what?"

"I don't know, Jace, okay? Just nervous."

"Okay." A twinge of hurt bolted through him, like a muscle spasm or a suddenly twisted ankle. He turned and stepped out of the house to find Carter and Carlos hauling a mattress up the ramp and into the truck. He joined them, getting the dresser and stationary bike loaded up. They made short work of the boxes and Belle climbed into the front of the moving truck with Carlos to direct him to the storage unit.

Only a ten-foot by ten-foot space, the three men—and Belle, who didn't just stand by and watch—got the dining set, the side tables that Belle said she'd bought in San Francisco, various home décor items, and several more pieces onto the truck.

It was only nine-thirty when he pulled up along the curb in the part of town called Monkeytown. Jace wasn't sure how the different neighborhoods had earned their nicknames, but everyone in Gold Valley knew them. The homes here had been around long enough to have tall, mature trees. Belle had two standing watch over her front yard.

The driveway and sidewalks had been cleared of snow, and the single garage door lifted easily. Someone had recently painted the house a neutral gray, making the gleaming white shutters stand out. With still a couple feet of snow on the ground, he couldn't tell the condition of the lawn, but he suspected someone took care of it. The house had that feel about it.

He followed Belle through the front door while Carter and Carlos started getting out the ramp on the truck. Everything inside had been redone. There wasn't a stitch of carpet and the walls were a blank slate for someone like Belle. The living room, kitchen, and dining nook shared the space, with a hall branching toward the left.

"Two bedrooms," Belle said, the first thing she'd said directly to him since telling him she was nervous. "Do you like it?"

All at once, Jace knew the root of her anxiety. "Of course I like it. It's bright and everything looks new." He thought of his newly remodeled place. He hadn't thought he'd like the white cupboards and laminate wood floors. But he did. And new paint and carpet in the living room and bedrooms seemed like a small change that made a huge difference. Even his loft seemed brighter with a fresh coat of eggshell-colored paint and bright blue curtains adorning the window.

He glanced through the big windows that overlooked the backyard. "Backyard's fenced. You could get yourself a dog." He smiled at her, but she scrunched up her nose.

"A dog?"

"Sure. One of those little ones. Shipoo or something."

She stared at him for a moment past comfortable, then laughed and laughed. The sound of it infused his soul, and Jace knew he was in real danger of falling all the way in love with Belle. His fingers twitched with the urge to touch her hair, hold her close, skim her skin with his lips.

"I can't believe you know breeds like shipoo. Don't ranchers have border collies and Labrador retrievers?"

"Sure." Tom had a Labrador retriever, and though Jace wanted a dog, he felt guilty leaving it all day while he worked. "Doesn't mean I don't know about other breeds." He took a breath and released it. "This is a great place, Belle. I think you'll like it here. And it's a lot closer to your office."

"Farther from the ranch, though." She dropped her gaze to the ground as an explosion of happiness burst in Jace's chest.

"We have cars," he said.

She beamed at him, and closed the space between them. She tucked her arm in his. "What if I got a cat?"

"A cat?" Pure horror snaked through him. "I don't know about that, Belle…. Cats might be a deal-breaker."

She narrowed her eyes. "A deal-breaker?"

"For me. I don't know if I can be with someone who prefers cats over dogs." He said it as seriously as he could, enjoying the confusion on her face and fear in her eyes. "I'm kidding, sunshine. You want a cat, get a cat."

"But you don't like cats."

"I prefer dogs. Cats are fine."

"Fine means not fine."

"Only to women." Jace threw her a wink as he opened the front door. "Now let's get this thing unloaded and the house set up so we can go eat. I skipped breakfast and I'm starving."

"Jace." The childlike quality of her voice stopped him.

"Hmm?" He faced her as the doorway framed them.

"Thank you." She stretched upon her tiptoes and kissed him. This time he felt the passion and power in her touch that he'd experienced previously.

"Happy to help," he said, his voice a bit hoarse. "Movin's hard."

Belle ducked her head and fiddled with her fingers. "Not just that," she said. "Thanks for pushing me to find a place of my own."

His chest tightened; an alarm began whining in the back of his head. "I didn't do that. Never even mentioned it."

"You didn't have to," she said, finally lifting her gaze to

his. "So thank you." She stepped out of the house and bounced over to the other two men. She gave them both a quick squeeze and started directing them where to put the items they'd last loaded.

Jace's lungs tangled with his intestines. He hadn't said a word to Belle about finding her own place. Not even one time. He didn't know how to feel. He didn't want to be responsible for her nervousness, her unhappiness, if she didn't like where she lived. He didn't want her doing things just to please him, because that made her feel unauthentic. Like she wasn't being the Belle Edmunds she was, but the Belle Edmunds she thought he wanted her to be.

No, Jace didn't like that she'd found a place of her own because of him. Not one little bit.

CHAPTER 13

"Thanks, guys." Belle's emotions lingered so close to the surface, her voice stuck in her throat and she couldn't say much more. Carter and Carlos climbed into the now-empty moving truck and rumbled off down the street.

Jace remained inside, unloading boxes. She stood in the driveway, her arms clenched across her chest, and looked around her new neighborhood. The houses on this street seemed well cared for. The driveways were clear, the trees tall, the homes in good repair.

You'll be happy here, she told herself. She'd felt it the first time she'd looked at this place. Knew she could be happy here—if she'd let herself. Truth was, she wasn't sure she could support herself in Gold Valley. She worked for the design conglomerate, because she got a small percentage of their profits whether she had her own clients or not.

But she really wanted to branch out on her own. She

had plans for the second bedroom. Plans to make it an office where she could design for her own clients. But in order to do that, she'd have to quit at the firm. She couldn't ethically take their clients and make them hers. And she couldn't quit until she finished the jobs she'd contracted. Horseshoe Home, Rimrod Lodge, and the Flat-head Lake contracts still had months of work to be completed.

"You gonna stand out in the cold all day?" Jace called from her front door.

She took one last look around before heading up the sidewalk. "Let's go to lunch," she said.

He hooked his thumb over his shoulder. "Still lots to do in there. I don't mind staying to help."

"We got the bed set up, and the furniture in place. It's just clothes and dishes and décor. I can do it later."

Or not, Belle thought. She just wanted to relax for a few minutes. "I thought you said you were hungry."

"Yeah, let me grab my keys." He ducked back into the house, and a wave of gratitude for him washed over her. Those emotions broke the surface, and tears pricked her eyes.

"Hey, what's wrong?"

"Nothing." She wiped her face quickly and looked up at him. "Just…grateful for you." A smile broke onto her face though she still felt like crying.

Jace's concern melted into something else. She loved the softness he carried when he let himself unwind. Though he was big, and strong, and tough, he possessed a beautiful compassionate heart, a soft touch, and a truckload of passion.

He tucked her into his side. "Where do you want to eat?"

"Pancakes?" she suggested.

He groaned, which elicited a giggle from Belle. "Kidding. How about that Italian restaurant? Migliano's? I haven't been there in ages."

"Are they open for lunch?" Jace asked. "I thought they were just open for dinner."

"No, I think they're open for lunch on the weekends."

"Let's try it." He pressed a kiss to her temple and didn't relinquish the hold on her body as they moved down the sidewalk to his truck. As Belle buckled her seatbelt and watched Jace stride around the front of the vehicle, she was struck with the realization that she'd done the right thing. A peaceful, happy feeling flowed through her from top to bottom and left to right. She couldn't help smiling, though those pesky tears pressed so close to the surface. But she didn't care. It was okay to cry because she'd done the right thing.

———

Belle's chest lifted with the quick intake of breath. Everything lately made her so emotional. The simple act of putting her own decorations on her own walls—well, her rented walls—brought her supreme satisfaction. She hadn't realized how trapped she felt inside her parent's house.

She enjoyed church with Jace—especially the part where

he came back to her house and made her a late lunch. After that, he pulled her close to him on the couch and kissed her soundly. She definitely enjoyed that part.

She'd spent a couple of days out at the ranch early in the week. The painting in the last cowboy cabins was going well, and should be finished by the end of next week. The carpets and curtains had been installed in half of the cabins, with the remaining structures expected to be finished from top to bottom five weeks from now, right on schedule.

She spent Wednesday at the Rimrod Lodge, where all the measurements had been taken, and double-checked, and recorded. She'd spent Thursday entering the orders for the new tiles that mimicked hardwood, the carpet, and the wall-paper. She loved the design Tilly had chosen, and Belle couldn't wait to see it in the guest rooms. The artwork would be ordered in a month or so when the rooms were mostly done, as would the new light fixtures.

After dialing Tilly and getting no answer, Belle left a message. "I'll stop by on Monday morning—after check-out, of course—to confirm the furnishings for the front lobby. I think you're going to love them."

Then she tossed her purse over her shoulder and picked up the lunch she'd packed for herself and headed out to her car for the long drive to Flathead Lake. She'd booked a room at the Hotel and Spa—as well as a facial and a full pedicure. She often stayed as a guest in the hotels she'd been hired to redesign, and for the first time since she'd booked the job, excitement danced through her at the idea of driving to Flathead Lake.

She sang along to the radio as she crossed the Native American reservation and continued north around the tip of the lake to the hotel. The owner knew she was coming, as evidenced by her overly friendly greeting at check-in and the local, gourmet chocolates on the desk in her room.

She took in the details of the standard guest room. Worn carpet in a bland shade of brown that would have to be replaced. She understood why a darker color had been chosen, but she also envisioned a brighter, more welcoming room with carpet the color of oatmeal. In fact, she'd just seen a dark-flecked cereal-colored carpet in her catalog a couple of days ago. It would be perfect here.

The wallpaper felt like sandpaper, and her fingers itched to pull it back and see what was hidden beneath. Maybe she could texturize and paint the walls a soft blue, or maybe gray, or perhaps peach. Depending on the shape of the sub-wall, anything was possible. If it turned out that painting couldn't be done, she could at least update the wallpaper to something from the last decade.

The sofa had seen better days and the light fixtures functioned, but neither added aesthetic value to the room. And guests noticed things like that. She lifted the cushion on the couch to find a sleeper sofa, but she knew she could do better.

The desk, bureau, wardrobe, and television were standard. She wouldn't touch them unless they needed repair. Well, maybe she'd put in new smart TVs. Something that could connect to a phone or a computer or a camera.

"And charging ports," she murmured as she pulled her phone out and couldn't find anywhere to plug it in.

Little things made all the difference. Belle knew this, had lived and breathed it for five years in Sacramento. She changed out of her work shoes and into a comfy pair of boots. If she had to drive two hours to her remodel, she might as well check out the local attractions.

Outside, the early April wind chafed her face, but it wasn't as bitter and biting as it had been a month ago. She wandered past the town hall building, which stood three stories tall and boasted a library on the third floor. The fire station sat next door, with a park beside that.

With the tantalizing smell of chocolate in her nose, she entered a candy shop. A man greeted her with a smile. "Let me know if you need anything."

"Something with caramel and nuts," she mused as she searched the candy cabinets. "Pecans, maybe. You have anything like that?"

"Sure, right here." He pointed to the mounded chocolate on the second shelf. "Dark or milk chocolate?"

"One of each, please."

He selected her treats while she moved on to an array of caramel apples. "And one of these. The one with white chocolate and crushed cookies."

"Sure thing." He removed the apple from the case. "Would you like me to slice this?"

"Yes, that would be great," she said. "I'm staying at the lodge, and don't have a knife."

He used a fancy tool to neatly core and slice the apple at

the same time, and Belle thought life couldn't get any better. Well, she knew exactly how it could be better—if Jace were by her side, choosing his own sweets to enjoy later.

"Where's the best place for dinner?" she asked.

"That would be Stewart's," the man said. "Assuming you like steak." He rang up her purchases. "If you prefer Mexican, you should try Paco's Tacos. Best tacos in the state. And we have a great Native American food truck that circles the lake. It's Saturday, so they'll be up here tonight. Fry bread and nachos you won't soon forget."

Though she'd eaten her sandwich only an hour ago, her stomach rumbled with the want of something fried. "Where does that food truck stop?"

───────

Jace's phone buzzed from somewhere inside his cabin. He'd worked well into the night to ensure everything would be ready to move the herd on Monday morning—including taking care of ranch responsibilities for the few cowboys remaining behind, shoeing the horses for their trek, and checking the lower pastures to make sure the snow had melted enough to put livestock out to graze.

He rolled over, thinking only one of two people would call him. Tom or Belle. Okay, maybe three—his mother. He only wanted to talk to one of them, and as the buzzing stopped, he wondered if Belle had been on the other end of the line.

Several moments later, right when he'd started to doze

again, his phone emitted a shrill beep. He'd gotten a message. Tom or his mother then. Belle would just call back.

Sleep claimed Jace again—at least until someone with very large hands practically knocked down his front door. He shot to a sitting position as Landon called, "Jace! You in there?"

The doorknob rattled as Jace stumbled to his feet and wiped his eyes. He made it to the front door without ramming into anything too dangerous, and whipped open the door, fully awake. "Landon?"

"My sister called. I couldn't make out a lot, but I got enough to know she called you and couldn't get ahold of you."

The buzzing phone. Jace cursed himself for not checking it. "What does she need?"

"I don't know. She wanted me to come get you."

"Where is—?" Jace's blood ran cold. "She went to Flathead Lake yesterday." He reached for his boots, which he'd kicked off by the front door when he'd finally made it home in the middle of the night.

"You think somethin's wrong?"

"I'll call her." If he could find his phone. He finally located it on the dresser, plugged in as usual. Sure enough, Belle had called twenty minutes ago. He rang her back.

"Hey," he said. "What's wrong?"

"H—" Her voice broke through the bad connection. "... on the side of the road."

"I can't hear you, sunshine. Can you hear me?"

156

"Barely," she said. "I'm in Flathead Lake, right? Well, my car—"

Frustration pooled in Jace's ears. "Can you text me where you are?" With the pieces he'd gotten, she had to be on the side of the road near Flathead Lake. But that place wasn't exactly small, with at least half a dozen touristy towns and miles and miles of shoreline. But there was only one way in and out.

Nothing came through the line, and Jace checked the call. Still connected. As he contemplated what to do, the line went dead. "Okay, she's stranded in Flathead Lake. Something's wrong with her car. She's gonna text me her location." He hoped. "I need you to stay here and make sure Ty gets the saddles ready for Monday. And Nelson should be packing food for two dozen men for a week. And—"

"I know what they need to get done, Jace. You go." Landon's bright green eyes reminded Jace so much of Belle, especially when he worried about something.

"Right." Jace grabbed his cowboy hat and stuffed it on his head. "I'll be in touch with you. Keep your phone nearby."

Landon held it up in response, and Jace swiped his keys from the dresser. He checked his phone every five minutes as he drove down the canyon and through town. Belle never texted. Once out of town and on the highway, Jace drove faster than he ever had before.

An hour into the two-hour drive, his knuckles ached with the unrelenting tension he kept on the wheel. His phone still hadn't made a single sound, and he'd checked it multiple times. Even had it plugged into the portable charger that connected to his cigarette lighter.

Finally, as he exited the Flathead Indian Reservation and passed through a little settlement, his phone chirped. He swiped it from the seat and saw Belle's name.

One word: *Lakeside.*

Relief and determination dove through him. He knew where Lakeside was, and he'd be there in forty-five minutes. He dictated as much to her and hit send. But the arrows just bobbed around each other, and the text didn't go through.

Annoyed yet grateful for modern technology, Jace focused on driving. How hard could it be to find someone in Lakeside? Rain splattered the windshield, and Jace's spirits got doused too. It would be harder in the rain.

Hard, but not impossible.

CHAPTER 14

*J*ace crawled down the road running through Lakeside. If he blinked, he'd pass the bulk of the little lakeside town. And he'd already gone up the street once and come back. He hadn't seen Belle's car. The white church on his left then the gas station. Then nothing but a few stores and miles of Montana tundra and the lapping waters of Flathead Lake that moved into frozen ice.

Maybe someone had seen her. He pulled into the gas station and went inside. "Excuse me," he said to the clerk. "My friend called me with car trouble. Tall woman. Auburn hair. Green eyes. You seen her?"

"Yeah, she came in a while ago." The woman cocked her head to the side. "Asked if there was any place to get coffee. I told her Glacier Perks." She pointed down the road. "Just down that way."

"Thanks." Jace flashed her the brightest smile he could manage. Once in the parking lot at the coffee joint, he still didn't see Belle's car, which made sense if it had broken down. One step through the door, and he found her.

Her eyes met his, and utter relief spilled from her expression. She bolted to her feet and strode toward him. "I couldn't get any of my texts to go through, and I didn't—"

"Shh." He met her halfway and crushed her to him in a tight embrace. He hadn't realized how important she was to him until that moment. Sure, he liked her. Liked talking to her and kissing her. Liked spending time with her, cooking for her, and planning a walk to the waterfalls once they melted a bit more.

But he knew now that she was more than that. She was *important* to him.

"I got one text," he said. "It said Lakeside. I asked at the gas station about you." He led her back to her tiny table, where a half-cup of coffee and more open cream containers than anyone had a right to drink sat on the tabletop. "Belle, do you even like coffee?"

That got her to smile, though it wobbled a little on her face. "I've had so much," she said. "I feel all hopped up."

He sat across from her and pushed the little cups into a pile. "Where's your car? What happened?"

"I pulled over to take some photos," she started. "I always do that for myself, to remind myself of a place when I can't see it every day. Anyway, I went back to my car, and it wouldn't start."

"Where is it now?"

"Out on this point. Point Caroline? It's a couple of miles."

"You walked it?"

"It's warmer than it looks outside." She gazed out the window as a fresh gust of wind hit it.

"Belle." Jace reached across the table and took her hands in his. "Why didn't you just stay in your car?"

"I didn't think anyone would find me." Her chin shook. "There are houses out there, but I knocked on a couple of doors, and no one answered. I think they must be summer lake homes." She took a sip of her coffee. "And it's not summer." Her emerald eyes met his, and he offered her a smile.

"You're a warrior," he said. "Let's go get your car."

"It won't start," she protested.

"I'll see what I can do." He tucked her against his side and took her to the passenger side of his truck.

———

Belle watched from the heated cab of Jace's truck. Watched as he popped the hood and bent over the engine. Tiny waves lapped the shore several yards to her right. She knew he'd fix her car. Fix her life. Fix everything, the way he always did. The man had hands made of gold, just as warm and rich and comforting.

It took him about fifteen minutes, but he emerged from

under her hood victorious. The grin he flashed her was as sexy as it was humble.

"You're amazing," she told him as she slid from his truck.

"Just helpin' out a beautiful lady."

She glanced around, her brow furrowed. "A lady? Don't see one of those."

He laughed as he slid his hands around her waist. "I got 'er started, but I have no idea if you can make it home. I'd feel better if we had someone look at it before we try to get all the way home to Gold Valley."

"It's Saturday," she said. "And almost evening. Nothing will be open."

A strange look edged his eyes. "Guess you'll have to extend your getaway weekend."

She shook her head. "I can't. I have a meeting on Monday morning."

"Me too." He exhaled. "Actually, I'm movin' the herd on Monday. I'll be gone for several days." He contemplated the sky, his mind obviously churning.

Belle's did too. She snuggled closer to Jace, stealing from his warmth as the last of the sun dipped below the horizon. "Maybe I can take it to a shop," she mused. "And just leave it. They can look at it this week."

"We'll go back tonight in my truck, and...I'll take you home. I can come get you for church tomorrow, and you can take me back to the ranch afterward. Then you can have my truck for the week. I'll be out driving the herd to the lower pastures anyway."

"And we can come back and get my car next weekend."

Jace beamed down at her. "It's a date."

With a rush of appreciation, admiration, and adoration, she kissed him. "Thank you, cowboy."

"Anytime, sunshine."

———

Belle filled up Jace's truck with gas on Friday morning and headed up the canyon. She hadn't seen him for days, and her heart pounded as she approached the ranch. He should've returned from moving the herd last night, and they'd agreed to get her car from Lakeside that afternoon. The mechanic had called yesterday morning, and everything had been fixed.

Thankfully, she had the money to pay for the new coolant tank and the serpentine belt. She pulled up to Jace's house, glad to have made it without getting stuck in the mud. The weather had been unseasonably warm the past week, and the snowmelt was soaking everything and making a mucky mess.

Jace emerged from his house, freshly showered and wearing jeans, a dark shirt, and his signature leather jacket. She drank in the sight of him as he moved toward her, a smile blazing in his eyes.

She scooted over on the seat, barely leaving him enough room to fit behind the wheel. He slid into the space, leaning down to kiss her before pulling himself all the way into the truck. "Aren't you a sight for sore eyes?" He scanned her black and white maxi skirt and fire engine red sweater. He took her hand in his and squeezed as he pulled his door closed and settled himself. "You ready for this drive?"

She groaned and laid her head against his shoulder. "Four hours in one day. Thanks for taking me."

"Of course."

"I wish we had a transporter that could get us there and back instantly."

"I don't mind driving."

"Of course you don't." She sighed. "I've always found it a waste of time."

"It's a great time to think."

"Okay, we'll agree to disagree."

He chuckled, but it faded quickly. "Do you think we'll do that a lot? Disagree and then agree about it?"

The way he spoke, it sounded like he was thinking long-term. Ashley's advice boomed through her brain. Belle already knew he was. It didn't upset her, necessarily. Since he'd kissed her, they'd leveled off there, getting to know more about each other's likes and dislikes, dreams and ambitions.

But knowing that every conversation contributed to his overall commitment to her brought a level of fear she didn't quite understand.

"I have land in Lakeside." He shrugged. "Well, my dad does. He apparently went about buying up land for a while there."

"Why's that?"

"He said he wanted us to have somewhere to live once

we left the ranch. You live there your whole life, and…then you have to leave when you retire."

"You think you'll work the ranch your whole life?"

"Yep." He glanced at her. "Does that bother you?"

"What? No. You're a rancher. And you're good at it. But I see your point about not having somewhere to live once you finish working at Horseshoe Home."

"My dad took good care of us."

"Where else does he have land?"

"I'm not sure. I just remember Lakeside for some reason."

The rest of the drive passed with easy conversation, and Belle decided she liked road trips just fine—as long as Jace was sitting next to her. The drive on the way home—after they shared a buffalo burger in Lakeside and Jace drove her past the empty wilderness he apparently owned—was filled with her own thoughts. She usually hated being alone with her thoughts, because she rarely liked where they went.

But today, she didn't mind so much. She thought about Jace, and his hard working spirit, his willingness to get back up when life kicked him down, his faith and friendship.

When she got back to her house in Gold Valley, she sent Jace a text. *You're right. That drive wasn't so bad. Thought about a lot of things.*

He didn't answer, but Belle busied herself in her new office. With only a few weeks left on the Horseshoe Home project, she needed to speed up the timelines of the other renovations she'd committed to so she could start her own design company.

She played around on her photo design software and ended up on a web browser, looking at other designer's logos and websites. By the time she realized how late it had gotten—and that Jace still hadn't responded—she was too tired to consider why.

CHAPTER 15

*J*ace couldn't sleep. Belle's text haunted him, ghosting up into his mind whenever he allowed himself to relax.

So he found himself walking the ranch by moonlight, the soft sounds of horse movement and the whispering of the breeze his only companions.

Oh, and his rampant thoughts. He wasn't sure which unsettled him more—being alone outside in the darkest part of night or Belle's text that she now liked driving so she could think. He couldn't figure her out. Was she just trying to make him happy? Prove him right? Show him she could get along with him?

He didn't want her to do any of the above. He wanted her to be authentic, be herself. And if she didn't like driving, that was just fine with Jace. But their differences obviously weren't fine with Belle.

Don't judge her too harshly, the breeze seemed to say, and

Jace paused. With his hands stuffed deep into his pockets to keep them warm, Jace tipped his head toward the stars. "What should I do?"

The thought of losing Belle made his chest cave in and his throat close. The thought of her changing what she liked for him enhanced the feeling tenfold.

"Should I talk to her about this?" He spoke aloud, his words streaming from him now. "What if she changes who she is and what she likes and then blames me? I can't live with her resentment. I won't do that to her. Am I over-reacting? Maybe she just wanted me to know the drive wasn't so bad."

Jace's words echoed in the empty night, and every muscle screamed with tension. "What should I do?" He whispered this time, desperate to know how to handle the situation.

Give yourself time. He'd been enjoying the slow pace of his relationship with Belle. It had taken him weeks and weeks to kiss her, and now that he could do that, he wasn't jumping to the next step. Truth was, Jace could still hardly believe that she wanted to be with him. Him, who still felt so broken sometimes, so unworthy of the attention of a beautiful woman like Belle, so stuck on what had happened to him in the past.

"None of that was your fault," he told himself as he turned back toward the row of cowboy cabins. His mother had assured him that she hadn't left because of him, or Tom, or their father. She'd said it so many times, Jace had started to believe her.

He didn't speak to Wendy, and her abandonment still cut too deep for the wound to be completely healed. But each day with Belle sealed the fissure in his soul a little bit more. At least he'd thought so. Now, he didn't know what to think.

I just want to stop thinking for a while. He climbed the steps to his front porch and entered his cabin, a new prayer in his heart. One that begged the Lord to give him the gift of a restful, deep sleep.

When he woke in the morning—an hour later than usual —Jace stayed in bed and thanked God for answering his prayers and giving him the night of rest he needed. After helping to finish the chores of feeding chickens and brushing down horses, he met with Landon to begin planning the planting schedule.

The ranch grew all it's own hay for the winter, and they had seventy acres to plant on this year's rotation. Jace's father had kept a rigorous crop rotation on a six-year-schedule, and Jace planned to follow it. In the thirty years his dad had run the ranch, they'd never had to buy hay to feed their cattle, horses, and sheep during the long winter months. And that took careful planning, a lot of time, and dedication to field preparation and irrigation that would dominate Jace's life for the next six months.

When Tom stopped by to offer Jace a ride to church, he declined it, claiming he needed more sleep. In actuality, he didn't want to face Belle. Instead, he texted her that he wouldn't be at church today, but he'd see her in the morning when she came to oversee the carpet installation in the eighth cabin.

She didn't respond, and Jace got a taste of his own medicine. It burned bitterly on the back of his tongue, and he escaped the confines of his cabin in favor of the wide openness of the Montana wilderness.

He saddled his favored horse, Think Twice, and headed out into the sloppy, melting countryside. If the sun kept up it's latest relentlessness, he could be planting in two weeks. That hope buoyed his spirits, and he finally felt the cloud that had been following him for a couple of days start to float away.

When he got up high enough that the snow made it impossible for Think to keep going, Jace turned around. He didn't spend as much time horseback riding as he used to, and he realized he missed being in the saddle. Missed the expansive, blue sky and the clarity of thought that came when he managed to get away from all his duties, the expectations, the insecurities.

He patted Think's neck as the horse practically ran into the stable. The horse got a fresh sack of oats and a full-body brush down before Jace left the barn. He felt clear and bright and ready to deal with anything the ranch or Belle or God wanted to throw at him.

So when he saw Belle's red sedan parked next to his truck in front of his cabin, Jace's heart leapt in anticipation of seeing her.

"There you are," she said as he came up the front steps.

He startled, missed the step, and tripped forward. "I didn't see you there." In fact, he'd forgotten he'd even put patio furniture on his porch. Because he hadn't—Belle had as part of his cabin remodel. All the boys had hammocks or rockers now, and Jace had even seen a couple of them sitting on the porch, playing the guitar or talking with each other as the weather warmed.

"How long you been here?" He made it to the porch and headed in her direction. "What time is it?"

"Shouldn't the foreman wear a watch?" She cast him a playful look as he sank into the chair beside hers.

"I usually have my phone." He exhaled and closed his eyes as he started rocking. "But I left it here and took a radio with me. Sometimes the cell service isn't great anyway, especially up higher on the mountain."

"Are you feeling better?"

He reached for her hand, fumbled around until he found it, and squeezed. "Yep."

"Good enough to go for a walk? The waterfalls are beautiful today. It's not too cold, and I made blondies."

He opened his eyes and glanced at her. She indicated a plate of baked goods sitting on the table between them. "Blondies?"

"They're like brownies without the cocoa powder."

He balked at this information, a measure of disbelief tearing through him. "Isn't the chocolate the best part of a brownie? Why would you take it out?"

She smiled at him like she would a disobedient toddler. "These are good too. Besides, you said you didn't like chocolate. Try one."

Had she made them specifically because he didn't like chocolate? And so what if she had? "I will at the waterfall."

He stood and offered her his hand. "Let's go." His stomach rumbled, and he took a detour inside. "Did you bring lunch or just treats?"

"I ate lunch on the way here."

"Do you mind if I make myself something? Will you drive?" He reached for the bread and peanut butter.

"Eat away, cowboy. And I can drive, sure. If you'll wash my car when we get back. That road on the way in is a mud pit."

"Yeah, we'll put sawdust and gravel on it this week. Landon's in charge of that, actually."

"I didn't hear you confirm you'd wash my car."

He chuckled, finished his sandwich, and turned toward her. "Sure thing, sunshine." He grabbed an apple and a bottle of water and threw his lunch in a plastic sack. "All right, let's go."

———

He ate while Belle drove to the waterfalls. She'd hoped he'd come with her, hoped he was just overly tired and needed a morning off. Sure enough, he seemed his normal, subdued but happy-to-see-her self, though he hadn't kissed her hello.

She parked and got out of the car, pulling the sleeves of her jacket down to cover the backs of her hands. Several others had obviously had the same idea as Belle, as brightly colored sweatshirts stood out against the mostly brown and gray background at the falls.

"Wow, there's a lot of water." Jace stepped to her side.

"When I was here a few weeks ago, there was probably half this amount of water going over."

Belle nodded and took a deep breath. She loved the long row of waterfalls just north of the town of Gold Valley. In the height of summer, it would look like one long waterfall, but right now, she could still make out the gaps in a few spots.

"You wanna go down the path and around a little?"

"Sure." He slipped his hand into hers as they started walking, and Belle's worries calmed. She wasn't even sure why she'd been worried. Because he hadn't texted back on Friday night? Because he hadn't come to church? The man ran an entire ranch. Managed hundreds of thousands of cows and acres and two-dozen employees. He was smart, and hardworking, but he was human too.

"How's the car?" he asked.

"Seems to be running great," she said. "Thankfully."

"That's great news." He spoke quietly, almost so softly that Belle had to strain toward him to hear him. "I love it here." He leaned against the railing across from the falls, one of the best vantage points for viewing them. "Tom and I used to fish here as boys."

"I remember the first time my dad brought us to Gold Valley," Belle said, letting herself take a trip down memory lane as well. "Landon loved these falls. Loved the tall trees. Loved the mountains. I was…less enthused."

"Where'd you guys move from again?"

"Chicago. I was born there. I didn't really want to move. But." She sighed and stared across the distance to the falls. "I did love these falls. I remember thinking how it was like a mini Niagra Falls, which we'd visited the year before. My mom told me I could come here anytime I was feeling sad or missing a friend from Chicago."

Jace draped one arm around her shoulders. "And did you come?"

A smile caught on her face. "No. I never felt sad or missed anyone. We moved into our house and another ten-year-old girl lived across the street. We became fast friends, and I didn't mind living in Gold Valley."

"But you didn't love it."

"I grew to love it." She turned to find his face only inches from hers. "I love it now." She pressed her lips to his. "I'm glad I'm back."

"Me too, sunshine." He kissed her again, quick on the mouth. "Me too."

———

Belle's gaze always went to Jace's cabin whenever she came out to the ranch. She tried not to, tried to focus on navigating the worsening road conditions on the ranch. Whatever Jace needed to do to fix them, he needed to do it fast.

But his truck wasn't in front of his cabin. She pulled into an empty space closer to the lodge and reached for the boots she'd brought, which waited on her passenger seat. Her phone went off, a snappy rhythm she'd chosen for Jace.

At Tom's. When you get here, come on down.

On my way. She slipped on her boots and stepped into

the spring mess. At least the path running in front of the cowboy cabins was gravel. Tom lived way down on the end, several hundred yards past the last cabin, and she had to detour back to the sloppy, muddy road. Well, at least the boots she'd brought would be put to good use.

A black Labrador retriever the size of a small pony lifted his head as Belle gained the top of the steps. A quick blip of fear hit her, but the dog laid its head back down and closed his eyes. She knocked on the door, and Jace opened it a moment later.

She entered Tom's house, where both cowboys sipped coffee. Jace handed her a mug. "I only added a couple table-spoons of coffee." He flashed her a quick smile. "Just how you like it."

"You're the best." She stepped toward him, but some-thing about his rigid body language made her freeze. She cast a quick glance to Tom, who watched their exchange with extreme interest on his face.

"Tom says we can take his cabin off the remodel sched-ule." Jace shifted his weight to his back foot, putting a healthy amount of extra distance between them, and sipped his coffee.

"He doesn't want his cabin remodeled?" She glanced around and found custom kitchen cabinets, clearly the work of a master carpenter. Hardwood—and not the kind she could buy from the best distributor in the country—decorated the floor. She bent down and ran her fingers along the grain. "Wow. This is fantastic." She glanced. up. "What is this? Reclaimed wood?"

"From a barn they were tearin' down last year." Tom leaned against his already-granite countertops.

"Did you do this?" She straightened and looked into his face for a brief moment before taking in the rest of the most luxurious cabin she'd ever been in—including some up in the exclusive cabin community on the mountain.

"Yeah." Tom followed her into the living room, which had the same floors as the kitchen. "I did the bookcases last year, and I finished the basement over Christmas."

"This place has a basement?" None of the other cowboy cabins had sported one of those.

"Tom's house isn't technically a cowboy cabin," Jace said. "We don't normally have married cowhands livin' on the ranch."

She spun to face him. "You don't?" Her mouth felt like she'd sucked on cotton balls all night. "What about—?" Her gaze flew to Tom and back to Jace, both of whom wore a mask of stone. Her heart banged against her breastbone so hard she thought they could see it. She couldn't believe she'd almost asked them what would happen to them once they got married.

She turned away as fast as she'd faced him, her thoughts and emotions tangling in a complicated web. Maybe Ashley's advice about this relationship only ending in marriage for Jace had penetrated Belle's mind more deeply than she thought.

Or maybe she was falling in love with Jace, and the ideas of marriage and where she'd live with him belonged solely to her.

"I have to go," she said.

"Wait a second," Jace called after her, but she didn't. She burst through the front door and gulped the still-chilly air. She leaned against the railing, not even startled when the dog came over and put his icy nose on her fingers. Instinctively, she stroked his head, taking comfort from his presence.

Jace stepped next to her. "So...you okay?"

"Why does Tom live on the ranch if he's married?"

"When my dad got injured about...oh, 'bout eighteen months ago now, he retired. Rob made me the foreman and I moved into my dad's cabin. It's bigger, as I'm sure you've noticed. I was raised in that cabin, too. It feels like home."

"Oh, so the foreman can be married and live at the ranch?" She felt his heavy gaze on the side of her face, and for the first time, she wished she had a cowgirl hat to use for the duck-and-cover technique she'd seen Jace do several times.

He chuckled. "Oh, so that was what you're worried about." His arm snaked around her back, his fingers gripping her waist and pulling her into his side. "You thinkin' about marryin' me?"

She adored the teasing quality of his tone, but the air suddenly seemed like sand, and she couldn't expel it from her lungs.

"It's okay if you are." He leaned against the railing too, the dog between their legs. "I've been thinkin' about marryin' you."

"You have?"

He sighed, his gaze singular on the horizon. "Little bit," he admitted. "Tom lives here, because this was an unused building and Rob loved my father. So when Dad asked if Tom could live here with his wife, Rob said yes. We could probably knock it down and use the land for hay, but well, Rob takes care of his men."

Belle's mind whirred, but she didn't settle on any one thought. She couldn't. She finally said, "So Tom doesn't need his cabin remodeled. I've put that in the budget." She took a breath, removed herself from Jace's side-hug, and stepped away from the dog. "I'll need to re-work that. See where we can spend the rest of the money. Or maybe the ranch would want to recoup the funds?"

"I'll talk to Rob." He looked at her with curiosity. "Should we get over to cabin eight? Caleb's probably wondering where we are by now."

"Sure, yeah." She followed him down the steps and driveway to the rutted road. She took his hand after they'd gone a few paces side-by-side. "I may have thought about us being married."

He squeezed her fingers in response, but she caught the handsome smile as it carved its way across his features. Warmth and happiness filled her with that smile and her next step contained a bounce she hadn't experienced in a while.

CHAPTER 16

After the conversation at Tom's, Belle dominated Jace's thoughts. He thought of making her pancakes on the weekends, after she woke up next to him. He thought about what he'd wear to his wedding—definitely not the navy pinstripe suit Wendy had picked out for him. He thought about building a life with Belle, maybe a life with children.

Jace nicked himself shaving as he pondered whether his sons would have her auburn hair or his dark locks, or whether their daughters would have her green eyes. He hoped so. He loved her green eyes.

As a trickle of blood wept down his chin, he stared at himself. "You don't love her," he told his reflection. He didn't say the next word on his mind— *yet*—but it lingered in the silence around him.

He shook his head. He couldn't fall in love with Belle, not yet. The fissures in his soul still felt too wide, and he wouldn't burden her with them. Still, as April melted into May, and planting season started due to some early warm weather, the feelings of love for Belle remained. He enjoyed holding her hand at church, making her lunch and cuddling with her every chance he got. Every time he kissed her, he fell deeper and deeper, and she seemed to match his passion with her own.

So one Thursday near the end of May, when Belle framed herself in his office doorway, he pulled her inside, closed the door, and pressed her against it in a kiss he couldn't contain. She giggled before deepening the kiss.

"I like coming out to the ranch," she said. "Especially when I'm greeted like that."

"Project's almost done," he murmured, tracing his lips down her neck to her collarbone. "Then what will you do? Just drive out to bring me lunch?"

She sighed and tilted her head back. "Maybe you'll have to come into town and see me." She stiffened, and he pulled back slightly. "Remember I told you I wanted to start my own design company?"

"Mm hm." His eyes drifted closed and he leaned his mouth close to her ear.

She shivered, which made him feel powerful and strong. "Well, I got the company licensed, and I'm working on a logo."

"That's great." He kissed her just below her earlobe. "Why you tellin' me this now?"

"Because when you come to town to see me, you can just come to my house, not my office."

He pulled away enough to examine her face for signs of distress, but he only found a shiny layer of joy. "I thought you still had months on the Flathead Lake project, and that Calvin wouldn't let you out of it."

"I'm hoping to convince him to take over by the end of June."

Jace's heart hopped over one, two, three beats. He wanted to skip June completely, and he thought he'd never be able to stomach living through those thirty days every year. But maybe with Belle by his side....

"I can come to your office," he said. "I'm capable." A flash of worry stole across her face so fast Jace could barely catalog it. He stepped back, his euphoria evaporating.

"But you won't have to. We have at least two more weeks in those barns—that's if your men can stay out of my way." She gave him a nervous smile.

"They have work to do." He didn't mean his voice to come out so solid, but it did, and Belle heard it. "And I don't need you makin' concessions for me."

"I'm not making concessions."

He moved to his desk and sat down, the payroll spread before him. His father had warned him that twice a month, Jace would hate being the foreman. The two Thursdays where he had to push paper and make sure the men got paid. And his dad had been dead on.

"Belle, I can handle coming to your office."

"I never said you couldn't."

"You implied it."

"I did not."

"I saw your face. I don't need you to change everything about your life, or yourself, for me."

Confusion scrunched her eyebrows together. "I don't do that."

Jace had let the things that bothered him—her saying she liked to drive so she could think, and her renting a place because she thought he wanted her to, and her making brownies without chocolate—fade. Let them go. Tried not to worry about them.

"So why'd you get a place of your own, then?"

"I…."

He'd kept his eyes on the papers on his desk, but now he lifted them to hers. He rose from his chair. "Why did you suddenly like driving, after you'd said you hated it?" He should stop, but he couldn't. "Why did you make a brownie without any chocolate?"

Her eyes seemed wild; they searched his with abandon. "I…it was nice driving that one time. I thought about *you*." Her chin shook. "I got my house for *you*. To show *you* I was as committed to us as you were."

"I didn't ask you to do any of that."

"When are you gonna get it, Jace? What else do I need to do before you'll take a leap of faith?"

"That has nothing to do with you. It never has." His throat felt tight, his chest downright clenched. "It's about me. And you promised me you'd give me the time I needed. You *promised* me that."

"I am!" She threw up her hands in frustration. "So what if I move while I'm waiting? So what if I liked driving home that *one time*? So what if I tried a new recipe?"

"I don't want you…I want you to be you, Belle. The Belle you are. I'm trying to fix myself." He ground the lump from his throat, but it caught and changed into a full-blown clog. When he spoke next, his voice sounded like he'd gargled with glass. "I'm trying to figure out if I can be happy with you, if I can fall in love with you. But I don't want it to be a warped version of you—the version you think I want."

She shook her head, a tear splashing down her cheek. "I'm not doing that."

"There is no mold," he continued. "I don't need you to try to fit yourself into my life. Either you will or you won't."

Her green eyes blazed as she wiped them. "Are you trying to push me away?"

"Of course not." His fists ached, his heart throbbed. "I—"

"I have to go." She tossed a brown paper sack in the chair across from his desk. "There's your lunch." She marched out, her back straight and her feet making angry clicking noises as she hurried away.

Jace sank back into his chair, the fight in him fleeing with Belle. He hated the sight of her back, hated watching her walk out on him. At least he'd had that luxury this time —Wendy hadn't even given him that.

Everything inside his body hurt, pulled wrong, twisted against itself. He swiped his hand across the carefully laid out paperwork, ruining the entire morning's worth of work. He didn't care. He needed to get away, find somewhere to think, talk to someone who could help.

Surprisingly, his first thought landed on his mother. Without second-guessing himself, he dialed her as he left the lodge through the backdoor so he wouldn't have to accidentally see Belle.

————

Belle held her head high as she left the lodge and scampered to her car. Thankfully, most of the cowhands weren't lounging around now that the weather had warmed and there was work to do out on the ranch.

She kept her emotion contained behind an iron wall while she made it down the newly fixed road. As soon as she turned onto the highway, though, with Horseshoe Home firmly in her rearview mirror, a flood of tears pressed against her will. She let them fall. Let his cold tone and harsh words ripple through her again, each time becoming stronger and stronger until they pulsed like a flag in a stiff wind.

She pulled into her driveway and all the way into the garage, pressed the button to lower the door, and waited to get out of her car until she was truly alone. She didn't have overly nosy neighbors, but she rarely came home in the middle of the day as it was, and she didn't need to start a wave of gossip about her heart being broken.

But that was exactly how she felt—like Jace had said carefully rehearsed words, words he somehow knew would wound her the most, cut her deepest, break her the hardest.

She moved numbly through her house, setting a pot of

water to boil for pasta. When she'd lost everything in Sacramento, she'd existed solely on spaghetti and meatballs and homemade macaroni and cheese for two weeks. Something about noodles soothed her when every nerve ending felt frayed, frantic, frenzied.

After changing into her pajamas—yes, in the middle of the day—she padded into the kitchen in her socks and collapsed on the barstool she'd painted a mustard yellow to match the new curtains she'd sewn a month ago. The water seemed to take at least an hour to boil, each minute while she waited amplified by ten.

She hated waiting. Was tired of it. She'd met Jace five months ago, and while they'd both thought about marriage, no declarations of love had been uttered, no plans for the future discussed, no conversations about what they each wanted from life had even happened.

"You knew he needed time," she admonished herself as the boil started bumping against the lid. She heaved herself from the stool and dumped in a box of penne. Stirring, her emotions bubbled like the water, steamed like the vapor, reached their breaking point. Her stomach swooped and her throat tightened as a fresh wave of tears unleashed themselves.

Evening found her in her office, her face washed free of all makeup and the pot of carbonara she'd made for lunch completely empty. She'd scrubbed the walls and primed them and painted them her favorite shade of blue. A light cornflower, it reminded her of the sky over California. She'd ordered a professional desk and a gorgeous rug to be delivered the following week, and now she swept white paint on the baseboards to complete the mini-makeover.

Staying busy was the only way she could keep her mind from stalling on Jace, so she didn't give herself even a moment of downtime. By Sunday morning, she'd slept barely four hours each night, but her windows all had new treatments, and her couch and loveseat had a dozen new throw pillows, and she'd sketched out a business plan that couldn't fail.

Well, at least she hoped it couldn't fail, and as she didn't have a whole lot to hope for, she seized on that.

She arrived late to church on purpose and squeezed herself onto the end of a bench where a family of six sat. No room for Jace. She hadn't called or texted, though she'd thought about it in the soft moments before she fully woke. He hadn't made contact either, and she often wondered if he'd been as tormented as she'd been over the past three days.

She had to believe he was. She hoped he was, prayed for it. But she didn't want to be the one to go crawling back. He'd been the one to express frustration with what she'd done. He could come to her.

But not at church, she'd made sure of that.

———

By the following Sunday, the ache of missing Jace clawed so deep, Belle couldn't touch the bottom of it. She didn't need to go out to the ranch to finish the reno on the barns. Her crew did just fine without her in their business. The account had been paid. She never needed to darken the roadway of Horseshoe Home Ranch again.

Every fiber of her being wanted to, though, and keeping herself from making the drive to see Jace had taken every ounce of her willpower. He'd texted a couple of times, once about her keeping the extra money for Tom's cabin and once asking her to please call him.

She hadn't. Couldn't seem to find the right words to say to him, though she'd never had a problem telling him what she thought before.

She stayed home from church so she could finish her office. She'd toyed with the idea of quitting the conglomerate outright, but hadn't yet found the courage to do it. *Maybe this week*, she thought as she adjusted the wingback chair she'd bought about two inches to the right. She immediately moved it back and stepped away from it.

An hour later, someone knocked on her front door. Probably one of the neighbors who'd noticed she hadn't gone to church. Maybe they had freshly baked bread or a plate of chocolate chip cookies. What she wouldn't give for something homebaked right now.

She opened the door and stumbled backward at the sight of Jace standing on her front porch.

CHAPTER 17

"You didn't call," he said, his expression tortured.

"You look tired, Jace." She gripped the door to hold herself upright. Her heart raced like it was a contestant in the Kentucky Derby. "You should go on home."

He crossed his arms and stared directly at her. "Didn't see you at church today. I was worried."

"I'm fine, as you can see."

"I can see that." He stepped across the threshold of her house, pressing into her space.

She didn't give him an inch. "I didn't invite you in."

"You opened the door."

"Jace—"

"I'm sorry, Belle, okay?" He dragged his pinky along her fingers but didn't hook it, didn't hold her hand. "I'm dying without you."

"Maybe you should've thought about that before you lectured me."

He ducked his head, and they stood close enough to embrace, to kiss. His breath wafted across her bare shoulder, but she didn't move. "I didn't mean to lecture you." He spoke with the gentleness of falling snow, and she wanted to lean into him, forgive him.

"I'm—I was just scared you were doin' things for the wrong reasons." His hands landed lightly on her waist, tiptoed around to her back. "Forgive me. I'm begging you. Please forgive me."

———

Jace didn't know how to live without Belle. The past several days had felt like he was living underwater without an oxygen tank. She let him collect her into his arms, but she remained stiff and unyielding. She hadn't thrown him out, and he figured the more time he spent with her the quicker she'd come around.

He sensed her reluctance though, and he didn't know how to deal with it. Not that he'd expected her to throw herself into his arms, but well, he had *hoped* she would.

"I've been talking to my mother." He rocked Belle left and right slightly. "She's been helping me understand some things."

"What sort of things?" She softened into him the slightest bit, and he kneaded her closer. He told himself not to kiss her, but his mouth touched her neck for a breath. "Jace, focus."

Humbled, he stepped away from her, because he couldn't think with the glorious, floral scent of her skin clouding his mind.

He cleared his throat. "She's helping me understand that it wasn't my fault she left."

Belle frowned at him, pressed further into the wall behind her, and crossed her arms. "I thought you already knew that."

"Knowing it and believin' it are two different things." He moved further into her house, disliking the conversation though he'd known what he was up against, had known she'd push him for answers. In fact, it was one of the things he liked best about her.

"You know I was just trying to make things work between us." She shuffled her feet. "Because I like you, and I felt myself falling in love with you, and I'm sorry that came across as me not being authentic."

The first part of her statement sent his heart palpitating, but the last part smothered his lungs in wet towels. "You have nothing to apologize for."

She glared in response. Cocked a hip. Lifted her eyebrows.

"Have you ever considered that what makes us great is that not everything works? That you can still be you and have your opinions, and so can I? That we can disagree and still like each other?" He watched her carefully so he could judge her reaction. She barely moved. "Belle, I like you too. I might even love you. But I also love that I can tease you, and shoot my best insult at you, and use sarcasm with you."

Her shoulders finally fell. "You might be onto something there."

He swept her into his arms, lifting her feet off the ground as he brought her mouth level with his. "Of course I am, sunshine." He touched his lips to hers, asking for her permission. She gave it, and he held her tighter and kissed her longer than he ever had.

———

"Mom, I'm running about ten minutes late." Jace dictated the text to his mother and hit send before tossing his phone back to the seat. Yesterday, he'd had a hard time leaving Belle once she'd forgiven him. And today, he'd driven straight to her house as soon as the ranch could release him. She had a comfortable couch, and since he hadn't been sleeping well, he'd fallen asleep in her arms. When he'd woken, he'd realized he didn't want to wake up anywhere else ever again.

The thought both terrified him and excited him. He ran his hand through his hair and resettled his hat on his head just as he pulled into the parking lot where he and his mother had decided to meet for dinner. She claimed O'Reilly's had the best chicken tacos in the country, and well, Jace liked a good taco as much as the next cowboy.

"Hey, Ma." He met her inside the front door and gave her a quick squeeze. "Sorry I'm late."

"I hope it's because you went to see Belle like you promised."

A smile sprang to his face. "I did."

Shock traveled across his mother's features, staying the longest in her hazel eyes.

"You didn't think I'd actually go see her." Jace folded his arms and scanned the Mexican joint so he wouldn't have to see his mom's face.

"I hoped," she said. "But sometimes you Lovell boys are awfully stubborn."

"Wonder where we get that from," Jace muttered. "These tacos have potatoes in them?"

"Don't change the subject. Tell me how things went with Belle."

They joined the line, which seemed to be moving forward at a decent clip. "All settled with Belle."

"That's what I get? Four words? I've never eaten out so much in my life as I have this past week. I've never seen a man so overwrought. And I get 'all settled with Belle'?" She made her voice deeper to mimic him on the last four words. "No way, mister. Tell me more."

Jace sighed and rolled his eyes, but secretly he wanted to tell her. He *needed* to. Talking with his mom these past several days had helped Jace in a way nothing else had. "You were right. She wasn't trying to be someone she's not. I can see that now."

"She said that?"

"A version of it."

"And what did you say?"

Jace stepped up to the counter and ordered the "famous" chicken taco platter for him and his mother. As they moved down to pay, he filled her in on the conversation and the general feeling he'd gotten from Belle.

"So now what?" his mother asked as she sat at a table for two in the corner. She passed out the tacos but didn't taste hers.

"What do you mean, now what?" Jace bit into his taco and moaned. "Wow, this really is the best chicken taco in the country." The saltiness of the potatoes and the spiciness of the taco created a little piece of heaven in his mouth.

"Come on, Jace. What are you going to do now?"

Jace took another bite and swallowed before he answered. "I don't know, Mom. I like her a lot."

"You don't love her?"

Jace ducked his head lower and finished off his taco. "I don't know how to do that, Mom."

"How to love someone?"

Jace gestured to the air. "Maybe, yeah."

"Yes, you do. You have a great capacity to love. What about Tom? Your dad? Your cowhands?"

"They're not women who walked out on me on my wedding day." The taco waged war against Jace's insides. "You realize that in eleven days, I could've been celebrating my one-year anniversary." He exhaled heavily and picked up another taco. "I don't know if I can...I don't trust myself to make the right choice. I don't know how I feel, and I don't know how to recognize real love."

After all, if he and Wendy had really been so happily in

love, wouldn't he have detected at least an inkling of her unhappiness? Wouldn't he have suspected *something*? But he hadn't. Her departure to sell luxury condos in LA had blind-sided him in the worst possible way.

"Look, Jace, I'm going to tell you something I haven't told very many people. Only one person in fact—your father." She wiped her mouth with a napkin and took a long drag from her soda. Jace paused in his eating to watch her, because he hadn't seen his mother look so nervous before.

"After I left, I wanted to come back almost immediately. But I didn't know how. I didn't know how to explain. And so I stayed away. I thought it would be better for everyone that way. I was wrong, and I know it now. Maybe Wendy feels the same way."

Jace growled. "I'm not interested in getting back together with Wendy. Ever."

"I didn't say you should be." She sighed and leaned forward. "What I mean is we're all human. We all make mistakes. Some are bigger than others. Some hurt other people along the way, whether we want them to or not."

Jace waited for her to get to the point, because he still couldn't see it. When she didn't continue, he said, "What's your point, Ma?"

"My point is she did something because she didn't know how she felt. And now you're *not* doing something because you don't know how you feel. But I think you do." She gazed at him steadily, the way Tom did when he had something important to say. Jace wouldn't tell Tom that, though. He still hadn't quite forgiven their mom for leaving.

"I really don't, Mom."

"You're just scared. You need to get past that, be honest with yourself, and then you'll know."

"You make it sound so easy."

"I didn't—"

"Jace?"

Jace glanced up at the woman who had said his name. Long seconds passed as he took in the blonde hair—now cut stylishly into a bob—and the blue eyes. The petite frame, the thin lips.

Wendy. Her name formed in his head, but he couldn't say it out loud. He glanced back at his mother, pushed away from the table, and walked out of the restaurant.

———

Belle sat up in bed, the device she'd been reading on falling to the pillow next to her. She'd fallen asleep reading—again.

Something had woken her, and she glanced around, trying to determine the time. Only nine o'clock. Pathetic. Still, she hadn't been sleeping well. The loud knocking came again, and she flew from bed and toward the front door. She checked through the peephole this time, and sure enough, Jace stood on her porch.

She opened the door. "Jace, are you okay?" He'd just left here three hours ago to meet his mom for dinner.

"Marry me," he said.

She giggled, cutting off the sound when she realized he

wasn't kidding. One hand pressed against her pulse. "You're not joking."

"Not joking." He looked exhausted and maybe like he'd been crying. But she couldn't imagine the tough, tall, thoughtful man being tearful.

She searched his face for more of an answer, but came up blank. "What happened at dinner?"

His features iced over. "Nothing."

Leaning into the doorframe, she folded her arms. "I'm gonna call liar on that one."

"Call it what you want. Do you want to marry me or not?"

Adrenaline poured through her in waves, almost drowning her. "Not like this, I don't, no."

"Okay." He turned and moved down her steps with the fluidity of a much smaller man.

"Jace, wait!"

But he didn't wait, and she wasn't dressed. She watched him get in his truck and tear through the neighborhood, absolutely baffled as to what had just happened.

So she did the only thing she could think to do. She got dressed, made a phone call, and got in her car.

CHAPTER 18

*B*elle sat across from Laura Lovell in a diner that served breakfast twenty-four hours a day. Jace would've been horrified.

Laura ordered coffee and looked Belle straight in the eye. "Wendy's back in town. We ran into her at dinner tonight."

The wind left Belle's lungs, knocking her backward into the padded seat of the booth. "Oh, wow."

"What did Jace do?"

"He showed up on my doorstep and demanded that I marry him."

Laura shook her head and wiped her eyes. "It's my fault he's all messed up."

"I don't think so," Belle said though she didn't feel a whole lot of compassion for the woman. She was Jace's mother, and he'd figured out a way to exist with her in his life. Wendy, he obviously had not.

"Is she going to be in town for a while?" she asked.

"I didn't talk to her," Laura said. "After Jace walked out, I stammered something about needing to go, and I left too. He's fast, that man. He was long gone before I even made it to the parking lot."

"And that was about seven."

"Right."

Belle added cream and sugar—and lots of it—to her coffee when the waitress brought it. Jace had likely driven around for a couple of hours before showing up on her doorstep. He'd been thinking, but he certainly hadn't seemed to be in the right frame of mind. She'd never pictured herself getting engaged to an exhausted, angry man while leaning into the doorway of her rental.

No, her ideas were much more grandiose than that.

"I've called him and he won't answer." Belle stirred and stirred and stirred her coffee.

"Give him a day or so. I'll try to talk to him."

Belle frowned. Maybe calling Tom to get Laura's number had been a bad idea. She didn't need a middleman to make things right between her and Jace. She needed to know what had triggered his impromptu proposal, and she'd gotten the answer.

"He said you've been helping him the past week or so," Belle started, hoping the prompt would get his mom talking.

"Yeah, just trying to make him see that he isn't the one at fault for what I did, or for what Wendy did."

"And that I'm not either of you, and won't abandon him."

"I never actually said that," Laura said. "He has to come to that conclusion on his own. I think he's getting there." She flashed a warm smile and Belle returned it. She didn't want to talk about Jace anymore, but thought it rude to leave before they'd even finished one cup of coffee. So Belle made small talk and sipped quickly, all the while a feeling simmering just below the surface that said Jace's mom knew more than she'd said.

———

"Please call me back," she said to Jace's voicemail for the third time on Wednesday. She'd called him five times on Tuesday, spaced a few hours apart. The stubborn cowboy had stayed silent.

Belle worked with her phone propped up so she'd see it if it rang or someone texted. She had a month left on the Rimrod Lodge remodel, and everything there was set to wrap on time. Calvin drifted by her desk, his gaze full of disapproval. Belle couldn't conjure the energy to care.

She'd asked if she could move her remaining projects to other associates, but he'd declined. Part of the benefit of the conglomerate was working on the projects she felt passionate about, and she couldn't just pawn them off on someone else, he'd said.

She understood his reasoning, even if she didn't agree with it. And she wanted her clients to be happy so they'd refer her to others.

Calvin had expressly told her she couldn't start any new

projects on her own, and she'd declared that she wouldn't be bringing in any more accounts. So they lived with the stalemate, and would for three more months until the Flathead Lake project completed.

Belle didn't mind so much. She enjoyed working with hotels, and she'd made a plan for how to contact several more in Gold Valley—and beyond. She could become a name in the hotel industry. Or at least her dreams told her she could.

But she also knew sometimes dreams could lie, or cause false hope, or create unrealistic expectations. As the days passed, she made her calls to Jace less frequently, until finally, by the time July rolled around, they'd achieved complete silence.

She found herself weeping at random times, and took to working at home so she didn't have to see the curious glances from her coworkers or explain anything to Calvin. One morning, someone knocked on her door, sending her heart right up into her throat.

She half-expected to see Jace there, but Ashley stood on the porch with her son, Jackson. "I heard about Jace," Ashley said by way of hello.

Belle's bottom lip quivered, so she just stepped back so the pair could enter.

"Wow, Belle, this place is beautiful."

"Thanks."

"How long are you staying here?"

"I'm meeting with the landlord tomorrow. We'd done a month-to-month lease, but I'm going to sign for six months and ask him about buying it next year." She glanced around at the work she'd put into making this house a home. "I like it here. The neighbors are nice. I'm creating the spaces I want."

"So you won't be living out at the ranch, then."

Belle shook her head. "I don't know what you've heard, but Jace won't even answer my calls." She shrugged like his behavior didn't affect her, but in truth, every breath felt like a hot knife through her chest. "We're not speaking at the moment, so I guess that means we've broken up."

"I heard his ex was in town."

"I heard the same thing. Haven't actually seen her."

"She's here visiting for a while. The girls at the park say she's giving her dad some real estate advice, helping with his firm, that kind of thing, and then heading back to LA by the end of July."

"Sounds great." Belle's voice sounded wooden, hollow, detached. She didn't much care what had brought Wendy back into Jace's life, only that he'd reacted badly to it. She'd been second guessing everything she knew about him, and she didn't like the feelings of resentment or anger than came when she wondered if he knew how much his silence hurt her.

"Well, I just came to check on you." Ashley smiled and gave Belle a hug. "You're doing okay?"

"Just fine." Belle covered over the lie with a false smile and a promise that she'd come to the Fourth of July parade the next morning. But as she padded back to her office after saying good-bye to Ashley and her son, Belle knew she wouldn't go to the parade. That meant being in public, and she certainly didn't want to do that. She'd learned to hide after the debacle in Sacramento, and she knew if she stayed off the radar long enough, people would stop talking. So she intended to keep her head down and her mouth closed until something more interesting came up in Gold Valley to gossip about.

———

Jace hadn't left the ranch in three weeks, hadn't spoken to anyone but his brother and his cowhands in that long, and had no plans to rectify either of those situations. Embarrassment more than anything kept him confined to his cabin, or the barn, or the lodge. He actually craved his payroll days, because then he could seclude himself in his office and no one found it odd.

Not that anyone had said anything to him, not even Landon. That had surprised Jace, but he didn't seek out the cowboy to detail how he'd performed a rage-a-holic proposal. He was actually relieved that Belle had been thinking clearly, because he hadn't been, and he'd tapped out at least a thousand texts to her. He'd queued up her phone number a dozen times a day.

In the end, though, he needed more time. More time to heal, more time to think, more time to just be. He didn't think it fair to her to keep going over there and apologizing just to do something equally idiotic the next day.

He'd realized through all his chats with his mom that he

needed more help than he was currently getting. The only person besides himself and Tom that knew Jace had started to see a grief counselor was the ranch owner, Rob. The hardest part about going to his appointments was the fact that the building sat right next to Belle's office. Try as he might, he couldn't stop himself from looking for her every time he went. He never did see her, and as the days passed, he wondered if he ever would again.

"Fireworks tonight?" Tom's voice came from the doorway of Jace's office.

"Can't." Jace didn't even look up.

"Yes, you can."

"Don't want to, then."

"You love a good rodeo."

Jace sighed and looked at his brother. "I don't want to go into town."

"It's one night. A big crowd. You won't see her."

"Which her?" Jace had done a little investigating, and he'd discovered that Wendy would be in town until the end of the month. With Tom nearby, Jace had no need to leave the ranch.

"Which one you worried about seein'?"

"Both of them," Jace answered honestly. "One messed me up, and I hurt the other. Not interested in seein' anyone, even those in the PRCA."

"Belle would forgive you if you'd just talk to her."

"What's the point, Tom? So I can hurt her again? No, thanks." He never told Tom what he and Dr. Fletcher talked about, but if the psychologist didn't think Jace needed to socialize right now, he wasn't going to.

"Who says you're going to hurt her again?"

"I do. She deserves...I don't want to hurt her again." There was only so much a person could take, and Jace didn't think he could strike out again and have her come back to him. This way, when he felt better, when he didn't want to leave town, when he spoke to her again, she might be able to forgive him. They could start over, the way they had before.

But if he messed up again? No, she wouldn't keep forgiving him.

"Please come to the rodeo," Tom said, his voice possessing a quiet kind of power that struck Jace in the chest. "You need to get out."

Jace let out a long breath. "What time you goin'?"

Tom grinned. "Seven-thirty. Come by the house, and we'll go."

———

When Jace showed up at Tom's that night, the front door stood ajar. The sounds of crying came from inside. But this didn't sound like Mari's frustrated wails or her furious sobs. No, this was Rose.

Jace hesitated, one hand on the door. "Rose? Is Tom here?" He didn't enter the house.

A few seconds later, Tom pulled open the door, his face wet with tears.

Concern spiked and panic rose. Jace had never seen his

brother cry—at least not since their mom left two decades ago. "What's wrong?" He scanned what he could see of the house, and it looked a mess. Maybe Mari had freaked out, broken things.

Tom ground the emotion from his throat. "Rose isn't feeling well. We're not gonna make it to the rodeo."

Jace's attention flew back to his brother's. "Tell me what happened," he said, because he knew something was seriously wrong here, and he loved Tom, Rose, and Mari. "Maybe I can help."

Tom glanced over his shoulder and stepped onto the porch, pulling the door all the way closed behind him. "Rose...." A fresh wave of emotion hit him, and he pressed his mouth shut as new tears leaked down his face.

Jace couldn't stand it, couldn't take the anguish on his brother's face, would've done anything to make it go away. "Tom, you're scaring me."

"We want to have more kids," he finally said. "It's not working out very well."

Compassion speared him, and Jace drew his brother into an embrace they hadn't shared in a long time. "I'm so sorry." The words weren't adequate, but Jace didn't have any others.

Tom's shoulders shook for a few seconds before he gathered himself together. "It's her third miscarriage since we got married." He pulled away and wiped his face. "We're worried the doctor will tell her she just can't have more." He stiffened, and Jace followed his gaze to the road, where Mari walked.

"I'll take her to the rodeo," Jace said. "Does she know?"

"Not yet. Rose just…it happened this afternoon."

"Should I take her?"

Relief washed across Tom's face. "If you could, that would be great."

"She can stay in my loft too." Jace tried on a smile, but it felt all wrong.

"I'll grab the tickets." Tom ducked back into the house, barely opening the door wide enough to squeeze his broad shoulders through.

Jace intercepted Mari, gushing about the rodeo. The almost-thirteen-year-old smiled at him. "Barrel racing."

"That's right." Jace beamed at her as Tom returned.

"Be good for Uncle Jace now," Tom said, most of the emotion wiped clean from his face. But when Jace looked at him, he felt it, saw it, experienced it as his own. And it hurt, hurt, hurt.

CHAPTER 19

*J*ace set the huge box of food he'd purchased at the concession stand in Tom's empty seat. "Here you go." He passed Mari her cotton candy and her grape-lime sno-cone, a "Scooby Doo" around Montana.

"Thanks." She focused on the horses circling the arena.

"It's about to start." He took a bite of his hot dog. "See the American flag?"

Sure enough, he'd barely had time to swallow before the cowgirl carrying the flag raced into the arena. The crowd stood as the announcer yelled, "Let's cheer for Old Glory!"

Mari clapped and Jace joined her. The National Anthem was sung, and the Pledge of Allegiance recited, and then the rodeo began with the bareback bronc riding. Jace had never been into the rodeo, but Landon adored it. He'd been a contender for a few years in his early twenties. Some sort of accident had ended his career, and he'd returned to Montana and Horseshoe Home.

But Jace liked nachos and hot dogs and soda, and by the time Mari's favorite event—barrel racing—came around, he felt sick. A smile curved his mouth. He felt sick for a good reason though, not because his heart hurt or his stomach was so twisted from his thoughts.

People streamed by on the sidewalk below the stands, and Jace caught sight of Landon. The tall cowboy would've been hard to miss. Jace stood and lifted his hand, calling out, "Landon!" before he could stop himself.

Two faces turned toward him.

One of them was Belle's.

———

Belle's heart stopped. Just completely stalled right there at the rodeo. She actually thought she might need to have someone dial 9-1-1, but then her most vital organ kicked into gear.

Jace stood about fifteen rows up, glorious and beautiful with the sunset creating a halo behind him. He wore clean jeans and a blue and white plaid short-sleeved shirt. His belt buckle glinted in the stadium lights, and that black cowboy hat he always wore made her fingers itch to take it off so they could feel his hair underneath.

Landon cut a glance back to her. "Belle?"

"You can go say hello." She juggled the sodas and popcorn they'd bought. "I'll take our stuff to our seats."

"You can't carry—"

"Well, I'm not goin' up there."

Jace stood as still as a statue, his gaze fixed on hers as his niece cheered for the cowgirl trying to beat the clock. Though dozens of people and dozens of feet separated them, Belle felt the heat from him, saw the desire in his face, tasted him in her mouth.

"I'm good," she told Landon as she tucked his candy bar in the crook of her elbow. "See you later." She hurried down the sidewalk, refusing to let herself look back at Jace. *He* had initiated this silence between them. He could break it. Or not. She wasn't sure which she preferred at this point.

You never should've let Landon talk you into coming to this, she lectured herself as she climbed the stands to her seat. *You don't even like rodeos.*

Landon didn't return before the barrel racing ended. He didn't come back during the team roping either. She stress-munched her way through an entire bag of popcorn and was about to start on his when someone finally came down the row toward her.

But it wasn't Landon.

Jace sat in her brother's seat, his eyes trained on the bucking bull in the arena. "Landon said he'd sit with Mari for a few minutes. He wants his popcorn."

She passed it to him mutely, then handed him the soda too. Jace got up and left without another word, and ooh, if that didn't make Belle angry. Why did the man have to be so good looking? Why did he have to smell so scrumptious?

Why couldn't she just admit they weren't meant for each other and move on? He'd obviously figured out how.

Jace returned a minute later. "He said not to eat his Kit Kat."

"I'm going to smash it in his face."

Jace did the oddest thing—he chuckled. The sound grated against Belle's nerves, the way it had as a teenager. "Maybe I should hold it for him."

"What are you doing?" she asked, the rodeo completely forgotten.

He finally looked at her, and she felt like she was coming home. She strained to keep a tight grip on her anger, but it fled at the sight of his sorrow, his pain, his determination.

"I don't like the rodeo," he said. "You want to go for a walk?"

"No, I don't," she said automatically, before her brain truly comprehended what he'd said. "Wait...you don't like the rodeo?"

His eyebrows went up. "Never really been my thing."

"I don't like the rodeo."

A spark of hope entered his dark eyes, lighting them from the inside out. "Why you here then?"

"Landon talked me into it. You?"

"Tom—Mari needed to get out of the house." He swallowed and choked, but regained his composure quickly.

"Are you lying to me right now?"

"No, ma'am."

Belle exploded to her feet. "Ma'am?" She growled at him, snatched her soda off the bench, and started down the row.

Her dramatic exit was foiled by the tightly packed people she had to step over, and besides, Jace followed right behind her.

She made it to the stairs and practically flew down them, Jace's cowboy boots thunking behind her at a steady pace. She strode down the sidewalk and under the bleachers, needing to get away from everyone right now.

Jace let her speed-walk until her stamina began to fail, until her frustration had bled out.

"So I won't call you ma'am again."

She stopped and spun toward him. "I'd just like you to call me." She got right in his face. "Why haven't you called me? Do you know how much that hurts?" She shook her head, her jaw tightening and her eyes turning glassy. "You know what, Jace Lovell? I don't care." She started to move away again, but he caught her arm in his hand.

"Wait."

"You let go of me right now."

He did, thankfully, because the storm brewing in Belle's body couldn't be tamed. She had no idea what she'd do if he didn't do exactly as she asked. She stared at him, her chest heaving.

"I haven't called you because I don't want to hurt you again."

"That's just something you tell yourself so you can sleep at night."

"I sleep very little, actually."

"You and me both, buddy."

He frowned, but it only increased the danger in his eyes.

"I've been seeing someone about my…problems. I didn't want to talk to you until I was sure I wouldn't hurt you."

"Every day that goes by without you talking to me hurts me."

"Belle," he said, but then fell silent.

Belle didn't know what to do. She'd thought about the moment she'd see Jace, be able to tell him everything that she'd rehearsed over the past couple of weeks. What came out was, "I love you, Jace Lovell. I promised you time, so you take as much as you need. But, please, can you call me some time?" Her throat spasmed; her chest recoiled; she swallowed hard. "Just so I can hear your voice and know you're okay." She blinked rapidly to keep the tears back. She didn't trust her waterproof mascara. "Okay?"

He nodded, the muscles in his throat so tight, she could see the tendons.

"Tell Landon I'm walking home." She moved away, half expecting him to grab her again.

He didn't. Instead, he called out, "Belle, you live too far away to walk at night."

"I'll be fine." She didn't turn around and didn't slow down. She couldn't believe she'd told Jace she loved him. Here, at the rodeo grounds, of all places. Now, when he hadn't given her the time of day for almost three weeks.

Through her tears and her pride, she could barely see. She made it a block before her muscles turned to sponge cake. She found an empty picnic table in the midst of the classic car show and collapsed.

Now what? she asked the Lord. She'd been praying for

two solid weeks for His help. Help to move on. Help to make it through another day. Help to soften Jace's heart. She trusted that God had done everything He could on her behalf, so she hauled herself to her feet and set her sights on her house—the only thing she could think to do at the moment.

Ten minutes and three blocks later, a truck idled up behind her. Her pulse skyrocketed and she didn't glance over. She increased her pace, her focus attached to a patch of streetlight about a hundred yards ahead.

"Get in the truck, Belle."

She paused at the sound of Jace's voice.

"No." She marched onward. "You can't just order me around. 'Marry me, Belle. Get in the truck, Belle.'" She shook her head. "Do you even know *how* to ask?"

The truck stopped, and she heard the door slam as he got out and closed it. His headlights illuminated the sidewalk where she walked.

"Belle, please." He caught her and hooked his fingers in hers for half a heartbeat before letting go. "I know you're mad, but it's not safe to walk home in the dark."

She paused, the fight leaving her body. "Fine, you can give me a ride. But I don't want to talk."

"Deal."

She followed him back to his truck and climbed in the passenger side. He kept his word and kept his mouth shut. He pulled into her driveway only ten minutes later, but she knew it would've taken her another thirty for her to walk home.

"I just wanna say one thing." He kept his head down as he spoke. "I'm real sorry, sunshine."

She didn't want to push him further away. In fact, she wanted to slide across the seat and kiss away his anguish. But the man had made the bed, and now he had to lie in it. She'd told him what she wanted. She'd proclaimed her love for him. He needed time—a blind person could see that.

Belle opened the door and got out of the truck. She leaned into the cab and said, "Prove it, cowboy," before slamming the door and entering her house.

———

Jace sat in his truck for what felt like an hour. Landon texted to say the rodeo had ended, and that finally got him to move. Belle wanted him to prove himself? He dialed her on the way back to the rodeo grounds.

She opened the line, but didn't speak.

"Hey," he said.

"Hey."

Jace had a hard time talking and navigating in the dark, so he pulled over. "I don't really have anything to say—which is another reason I haven't called."

"Well, maybe when you call tomorrow, you'll have thought of something."

"What if we go to the parade together instead?" Jace couldn't believe the words had come from his mouth. He hadn't been planning to go to the biggest celebration in Gold Valley. The park would be swamped with people, vendors, musicians, kiddie blow-up toys, and heat. All the things Jace usually avoided.

"Are you ready for that?"

"Are you?"

"No," she said. "I told my friend Ashley I'd go to the parade, but I don't really want to."

"What do you want to do instead?"

"I was planning on sleeping in and then puttering around the backyard."

"We were plannin' to do the same thing then." He grinned to himself, wishing she were there to see him. At the same time, he had no idea what he was doing—was he really going to start seeing Belle again? When Dr. Fletcher had asked him that question last week, Jace had shaken his head, his jaw clamped tight around his vocal chords.

Dr. Fletcher had asked why, and Jace couldn't answer.

But he couldn't keep hurting her either. He had some idea how much silence sliced, because when Wendy left and he couldn't get ahold of her for a few days, he'd practically hemorrhaged. But she'd been his fiancé. Belle was just his girlfriend—and she *had* turned down his proposal.

It was a lame proposal, he thought, a hint of embarrassment infecting his thoughts. He'd never wanted to go back in time to erase something more than he did that night.

"Are you listening to me?" Belle's tone reminded him he wasn't alone with his thoughts.

"I spaced out," he admitted. "What were you saying?"

"I was saying I don't think I'm ready to see you in person every day. So let's start with having a conversation where we both have something to say and we're both listening."

"So I'll call you tomorrow."

"I'll keep my phone nearby so if I'm napping, I can answer." She giggled, and for the first time in weeks, Jace's chest didn't feel like a bear had stomped on it. He hung up and hurried back to the rodeo grounds, where the crowd still steadily streamed from the stands.

Landon brought Mari over, then headed for his own truck.

"Did you like the rodeo?" Jace asked Mari.

"Yes."

"You like the bulls or the horses better?"

"Horses."

"You feelin' okay? Don't tell your mom I gave you so many treats, okay?"

She swung her head toward him. "Secrets." She grinned, and Jace chuckled.

"Yeah, secrets." He had some of his own, and though the evening had started out stressful—Jace's heart twisted for his brother's and Rose's loss—it had ended better than he could've hoped.

CHAPTER 20

$\mathcal{J}$ ace went to the parade with Landon, Caleb, and Ty. He didn't miss the way a gaggle of pretty girls kept eyeing them. He supposed he couldn't blame them—four cowboy bachelors sitting on their camp stools certainly drew some attention. Sure enough, one of the women came over during a lull between floats.

"How you boys doin'?" She twirled the ends of her blonde hair between her fingers. Jace watched his men to gauge their reactions. They often went into town on the weekends for a little rest and relaxation, and back in his early twenties, he'd joined them.

Landon glanced up at the blonde and back to the parade. He said nothing, leaving the task to someone else. Jace wondered what that was about. Last summer, Landon had led the boys in trips to Gold Valley for dancing and fraternizing with women. Jace made a mental note to ask his friend about it when they weren't in mixed company.

Caleb, a sandy-haired native of Gold Valley, smiled at the woman. "Just fine," he said. "And yourself?"

"Me and the girls were wonderin' if you guys will be at the dance tonight."

"Sure thing." Ty beamed up at her. "What about you, Landon?"

"Maybe," he said, looking again at the girl.

"Want to give me your number?" Caleb asked. "We can meet up later tonight." He glanced at Jace. "That okay, boss?"

He couldn't help grinning at the hopeful look on Caleb's face. Ty's too. "The day's yours, boys. Just come home in one piece." He nudged Landon with his boot, but the other man didn't look at Jace.

The parade continued, but Jace didn't see much of it— until a classic car cruising from one curb to the other bearing the banner "Suman Real Estate" rolled up. Wendy sat in the front seat, waving for all she was worth, like anyone here cared about their cherry-red convertible or their exclusive lots on the east mountain.

Every muscle in Jace's body tensed, but he employed some of the anger management techniques Dr. Fletcher had taught him. He met Wendy's eye and she visibly startled; her wave faltered; fear flashed across her face.

Jace lifted his hand in acknowledgement, more for himself than for her. The car continued past, and the next entrant in the parade blasted loud music for the high school's cheerleaders.

Jace catalogued the rate of his pulse, the steadiness of his nerves. Everything operated as normal. He'd just survived his first encounter with Wendy where he didn't want to walk away and punch something.

A smile floated across his lips, and he pulled out his phone to text Belle.

―――――

The Monday following Independence Day, Belle called into the office to tell Calvin she'd be in late because she had to go sign some lease agreements. She'd just entered the realtor's office just as her phone rang.

Jace.

A smile bloomed on her face. True to his word, he'd called every day for the past five, and she'd enjoyed their conversations. He told her about ranch happenings, and she updated him on the condition of her office.

He detailed why he hated sitting alone at church, and she told him she'd found a new escape—the library in town. When she told him she didn't remember Gold Valley having a library, he'd told her about it's birth in the Town Hall building five years ago.

He didn't push her to go out with him, and she never brought it up. For now, their conversations allowed her to have him in her life, and she felt like he was giving what he could. She'd promised him time, and each night when she prayed, she asked God to help her be patient. So far, so good.

"Jace," she said as she swiped on the call. "I'm just headed into a meeting. Can I call you back?"

"Sure thing, sunshine."

She smiled and said, "'Bye, Jace." She tucked her phone in her purse and glanced at the woman waiting for her. Belle towered over her by at least six inches, yet her meticulously styled blonde hair and shining blue eyes could put fear into a grown man.

"Are you Belle?" she asked.

Belle tried to smile, but the woman put off a seriously cold vibe. "Yes, ma'am."

She frowned. "Were you just talking to Jace? A Jace Lovell?"

Belle mirrored her frown with one of her own. She adjusted her purse strap on her shoulder. "Yes."

She folded her arms over the file she held in her hand. "How do you know him?"

"He's...well, I honestly don't know what he is." Belle forced a giggle across her vocal chords. "We dated for a few months, but now things have cooled off."

Way too much interest passed through the woman's expression. "Well, let's sign this agreement, shall we?"

"Yes, let's." Belle wanted to get her business over with and get out of the woman's presence. She was efficient, and she detailed the items Belle had asked about. Yes, she could landscape the backyard. Yes, she could paint the bathroom. Yes, she could put in a backsplash in the kitchen.

"I don't know if my father will want to sell in six months," she said. "But I'll try to push him in that direction. He's getting older, and he'd be better off just managing his multi-family units." The woman flashed a smile, but it came and went so quick, Belle wasn't sure it had truly manifested itself.

"Thank you." Belle took her copy of the signed documents and stood to shake the woman's hand. "I never got your name."

"Wendy Suman," the woman said, her blue eyes as hard as diamonds. "You're dating my ex-fiancé."

Belle's first reaction was to turn tail and run. Her second was to smile, and she seized onto that one. "Oh, we're not dating."

"But you said—"

"I said we dated for a while, but that things weren't serious right now."

Wendy cocked her head, that extremely annoying curiosity back in her eyes. "Why's that?"

Belle didn't want to tell her anything, least of all anything damaging about Jace. How dare she stand there like everything had turned out peaches and cream? Maybe for her. Belle forced a measure of kindness she did not feel into her words.

"Oh, I'm struggling right now." She tried to giggle but it came out like a hacking cough. "Had to move back home. You know."

Wendy's piercing gaze finally left Belle and she glanced around the office. "Yes, I think I understand."

"Do you live here?" Belle asked.

"No, I'm out of LA. Just here to help my dad get some things done that he's fallen behind on."

"Oh, that's so nice of you." Belle almost gagged on the sweetness of her voice. Her phone chimed Jace's ringtone from inside her purse, the two blips an indication that he'd texted. "Well, thanks for meeting with me. I have to get to work." She pulled her phone out and saw his name. "Yep, that's my boss." She flashed Wendy a smile without meeting her eyes and turned to leave the real estate office.

"Good luck," Wendy called after her. Belle didn't answer, didn't know how to. What could she possibly need luck with?

Once in the safety of her car, and with at least five miles between her and Wendy, Belle dialed Jace. "Oh, my water-falls," she said when he answered. "Guess who I just met?"

"Who?"

"Your ex-fiancé." She waited for his reaction, but he didn't give her one. "She's my landlord! Her father owns my house."

"Well, that's just unfortunate."

Shocked as she was, Belle could only laugh. "You should've seen her face when I said your name. It was like she'd seen her worst nightmare come true."

"She heard my name?"

"You called me right when I got there."

"She seemed upset?"

"Upset isn't quite the right word. Dismayed, maybe. Cold, definitely. She's not exactly a people person, is she?"

The silence coming through the line indicated that

perhaps Belle had said something she shouldn't have. But when Jace started laughing—and couldn't stop—Belle joined him.

"Meet me for lunch," she blurted out once he'd quieted.

"Belle…you're ready for that?"

"I am, cowboy," she answered with finality. "Are you ready to see me?"

"I've been prayin' for it, sunshine."

Giddiness galloped through her gut. "Great. I'll pick up sandwiches and meet you at the waterfall in…." She checked her dashboard for the time. "Forty-five minutes. Does that work?"

"Yep."

"See you soon." Belle hung up and rested her head on the seat behind her, only a thin stream of anxiety running through her. She loved him, she'd known it for weeks. She'd told him so. Now she had to trust her feelings, trust the Lord, and most of all, trust Jace, that they could make this relationship work.

CHAPTER 21

*J*ace pulled into the parking lot at the waterfalls. They roared over the cliff, creating that beautiful sound that reminded him of happier times. Now, though, he realized he could be happy again. Seeing Wendy at the parade and not wanting to run away had changed him, helped him turn a corner.

Dr. Fletcher thought so too, and Jace had been stewing over how he could get Belle to see him face-to-face. He had a lot to tell her, but none of it should be said over a phone line. So he'd made small talk about the ranch and other things of little importance.

Her car sat several stalls down, and his pulse skipped. Her declaration of love bounced through his mind, like it had been doing since the rodeo. He caught sight of her, a fast food bag dangling from her fingers, several paces ahead on the boardwalk leading toward the park on the other side of the falls. It would be quieter over there, more private.

He moved quickly, taking long strides to eat up the distance between them. "Hey, gorgeous," he said when he came within a foot of her. She turned, the bag of sandwiches bouncing into his leg, and stumbled backward when she found him so close.

He chuckled and latched onto her waist to keep her from falling. Their eyes locked, and Jace found everything in hers he'd hoped for. "I miss you," he whispered, leaning forward. "I'm sorry I'm, well, who I am right now. But I'm miserable without you. At least with you, I was getting better."

"You said you were seeing a doctor. That he was helping."

"He is. But he's not you. *You* help me. You make me feel like I'm worth fighting for. You make me, well, me."

She tucked her hair behind her ear with her free hand and grinned, her eyes shining. "I think that's the most romantic thing anyone's ever said to me."

"I guess sometimes the truth can be romantic, then." He rested his cheek against hers and took the deepest breath he could. Oh, how he'd missed the rosy-soft smell of her skin, the orange marmalade of her shampoo.

"I love you, Belle Edmunds. I want to spend my life with you. You make me a better man, and I want to be that man for you."

He heard the thud of the sandwiches as she dropped them, felt the thrill of her touch as she tiptoed her fingers up his bare arms and through the hair on the back of his neck, the rush of the breeze when she removed his cowboy hat and held it against his back.

He pulled back an inch to find her eyes already closed, her mouth slightly open and waiting for his. He touched his lips to hers, gently, softly, patiently. She sighed into him, pressed closer, and Jace had a whole new reason to love coming to the waterfalls.

An hour later, he lay with his head in Belle's lap, her fingers stroking a pattern along his scalp. It seemed impossible that such a fantastic, forgiving woman could love him. But he'd felt it in her touch and heard it in her voice.

He knew he still had a journey of healing ahead of him, but he also knew he needed Belle by his side to complete it.

"I finished Rimrod Lodge," she said, her voice lazy and low.

"That's great. How's Flathead Lake coming along?"

"Good." She sighed. "Real good. I paid for my house for the next six months, and I'm hoping to have clients of my own by the fall."

"That's amazing." He grinned up at her. "You're amazing."

She looked out across the park. "Jace, can I ask you something?"

"Sure."

"Do you believe in soul mates?"

He thought about her question, wondering why she needed to ask it now. "I believe in true love, yeah. I believe two people who love each other enough can work through anything, especially with the help of God." He shifted up onto one elbow. "I believe that you and me have the same goals. We both believe in God and are trying to be kind and hardworking. If we're not soul mates today, we will be one day. Might take work, but we can do it."

She cupped his face in her hands. "I love you."

"Love you too, sunshine."

———

Nerves rioted through Jace as he followed Tom and Rose to Silver Creek. They hadn't coped as well as they would've liked with their recent losses, and Tom had mentioned to Jace that all three of them were going to do equine therapy for a few months. "You should come," Tom had said. "I worked with patients in Texas. It really works."

Jace had taken a couple of days to think about it, and then he'd called Tom and asked when they were going. The very next day, and Jace didn't have as much time to prepare as he would've liked.

And he'd mentioned it to Belle, which only added to his anxiety, for reasons he couldn't name.

Silver Creek sat on a sprawling estate at the base of the mountain leading up to the cabin community. The green grasses spread in all directions, leading up to a beautiful, century-old building. Once they checked in there, Rose led them out the back, where several more buildings stood in the distance. To their left waited a barn and stables—and a tall, wide wrangler wearing a cowboy hat the color of snow.

Jace relaxed at the sight of the cowboy. Jace understood

cowboys, and horses, and the therapeutic center suddenly just became the ranch. He walked next to Tom, who held Rose's hand in his right hand while Mari trailed behind them all.

"Mornin'," the cowboy said.

Tom shook his hand and called him Owen before turning to Jace. "This is my brother, Jace."

"Owen Carr." The man smiled. "I hear we're all ridin' today. I've got my four best horses ready for you." He beamed at Mari. "You're saddlin' your own, Missy."

She smiled at him and stepped down the aisle to where a tall, black horse waited.

"I wasn't sure what you folks wanted to do." Owen glanced at Tom and Rose with compassion and caring in his eyes. "I can start you at the beginning, with saddling and horse care, or we can go straight to riding, since you're familiar with the animals." He lifted his hat and scrubbed his fingers across his buzzed hair. "Honestly, Tom, I feel like you should give the lessons instead of me."

Tom stepped forward and clapped Owen on the back. "Rose needs to start at the beginning. I want to do it with her." He cut a glance at Jace. "My brother...Jace, what do you want to do?"

"I'm already comfortable around horses," he said, his throat so narrow the words could barely come out. "But I've never looked at them as therapeutic. I'll start at the beginning too."

Owen visibly relaxed and gestured them forward. "All right, then. First things first. Horses can sense how a person feels. You have to be calm around them, isn't that right, Mari?" He passed the stall where she was just finishing latching the nosepiece on her horse. "Take 'im out to the arena when you're done," he told her. "Walk 'im until I come. I have a new game for you today."

She glanced up but didn't make true eye contact. "Mom?"

"I'm going to come watch in a few minutes." Rose gave Mari a smile and the girl used the bottom rung of the fence to swing up onto the horse's back.

"I've got Yellowstone, Kimchi, and Thomas Edison for you guys today." He looked at the three of them expectantly.

"I'll take Yellowstone," Jace said, and Owen waved him toward a brown and white paint horse.

"You're going to talk to him," Owen instructed. "You can tell him whatever you want. Then brush him down—avoid this one's right back leg. You can see he has an old injury there—and saddle him up. I'll be back in about a half an hour to take you guys out to the arena."

He led Tom down to the next stall, where he got assigned Kimchi and Rose took the last horse. Enough distance lingered between them that Jace could speak to Yellowstone and his brother wouldn't overhear.

But he had no idea what to say. The horse nosed his hand, and Jace ran his fingers up the horse's head. "Hey, boy," he whispered. "So I guess you already know that my fiancé left me last year. Can't imagine that gossip doesn't get around to horses too."

Yellowstone closed his eyes halfway, completely unconcerned with Wendy's departure. Jace smiled, the part of him that had held onto her abandonment for over a year withering, dying. "I've found this woman, Belle, and she's, well, she's amazing." He ran his hands down both sides of the horse's neck, mesmerized by this animal that stood so still and seemed to be listening so intently.

"She's patient, and kind, and well, sometimes she says things I just can't understand, but it makes us work, you know?" Jace was sure the horse nodded. He reached for the currycomb, but Yellowstone didn't have a fleck of dirt in his hair. He switched to a soft bristle brush and began stroking the horse down his chest and shoulders.

He continued to talk, to tell Yellowstone about the horses on the ranch, and his worries about Tom and Rose and if they'd be okay if they couldn't have babies of their own. Jace said, "I'd like a baby one day. Guess I better talk to Belle about that, huh?"

Yellowstone nickered, and Jace grinned as Owen said, "Seems like you two are gettin' along just fine. C'mon." He hooked his thumb over his shoulder. "I've got everyone out in the arena." He patted Yellowstone. "Oh, you've been spoiled today, haven't you? Ready to play a game, then?"

Jace led the horse down the way Owen had indicated, feeling more whole and more content than he had since Wendy left.

Belle called Jace twice before she remembered he'd gone to an equine therapy session with his brother. Half of her wanted to rush over to Silver Creek and watch the session, though Jace had asked her not to come. He wouldn't let her come to Dr. Fletcher's office either. Not that she really wanted to go. She just wanted to give him all the support he needed.

The half that wanted to fall back into bed won. She dozed for the next couple of hours, her thoughts tumbling over plans for reaching out to the businesses in the community that might be interested in a remodel and then spinning when she thought about designing and sewing her own wedding dress.

She woke when her phone rang with the popular lyrics of her favorite song. "Jace," she said when she answered. "How did it go?"

"So great," he said. "I'm going again next week."

She pulled her knees to her chest and listened to the bubbly, happy sound of his voice as he spoke about a horse named Yellowstone and a game they'd played where the horse kneed a ball back to him.

"So I have a question for you."

"Ooh, sounds ominous." She giggled. "I'm ready."

"I want you to meet my parents. Do you think we could go to dinner tonight?"

Belle's heart stuttered before it resumed beating at twice its normal speed. Maybe three times. "Sure," she croaked. "That sounds great."

He laughed, the deep timbre of it rumbling in her soul. "You sound like I just told you I was a zombie."

"I just wasn't expecting that," she said, her voice returning to normal. Thankfully. "We haven't talked about meeting our parents."

"Well, I've already met yours. Lots of times."

"I know your dad. Sort of."

"So, tonight? I was thinking we could try that new wrap station."

"Jace," she admonished. "Just because you could put anything into a sandwich and like it doesn't mean it's appropriate for dinner."

"I don't know what you mean."

His confusion was cute really. "That's a fast-casual place. You don't even sit down."

"Sure you do. There's tables and everything."

"You go through a line and order. I want to be served. I want time to talk to your parents."

"Well, that's…. Okay, so not the wrap station. What did you have in mind?"

"Hmm." She scooted to the edge of her bed and eyed the garment hanging from her closet door. "I just made a new skirt. It would be perfect for the American Bistro on Dover Street. *And* they serve sandwiches, so you'll still get what you want."

"I don't see how a skirt matters to a restaurant."

She laughed, glad when he joined in. "Well, cowboy, you'll see how tonight."

"I'll call my mom and dad right now." He exhaled. "What are you up to?"

"Oh, you know. This and that." She didn't want to tell him she'd been up half the night doing yoga and sketching the outline for her wedding dress, which had prompted her to sleep until almost noon.

"Can I stop by?"

"Are you already out front?"

"Maybe."

She giggled and said, "I'll unlock the front door." She hung up and made her way down the hall. She twisted the lock, and he opened the door in the next breath.

He scanned her from her bed-head to her bare feet, taking in the silk pajamas she still wore. "This and that? Looks like you just got out of bed."

"I did." She wrapped her arms around his shoulders and kissed him.

"Mm, I like that." He kissed her again, his strong arms and capable hands holding her in place against his body. He smelled vaguely of leather and horse, hay and lavender, and she took a deep breath of the cowboy she loved so she could carry him with her always.

CHAPTER 22

*B*elle took careful minutes to get herself ready that night. For some reason, her heart thundered and her ribs felt like prison bars. Jace arrived to take her to the bistro, and she twirled for him in her new red skirt.

"It looks hot," he said a devilish twinkle in his eye. "I like it."

She'd paired it with a black and white polka-dotted blouse that showed her shoulders and narrowed at her waist. He drew her close and traced his lips up her neck. "I like all of what I see."

"Don't ruin my makeup." She swatted at him playfully, and he released her with a chuckle.

"I've never seen you wear so much makeup," he commented.

"Rude," she fired back. "You're supposed to say how beautiful I look and that your mother is going to love me."

249

She hadn't told him about her previous meeting with his mother. She probably should.

He blinked once, twice. "You look great, Belle. My mother is going to love you." He delivered the lines with all the charm of a robot.

She rolled her eyes and picked up her purse. "Let's go. Did you look at that menu I texted you?"

"Sure did."

"Did you see the pulled pork grilled cheese?"

"I might surprise you tonight and not get a sandwich." He put his hand on the small of her back as she passed him and headed down the steps.

"I would be surprised by that."

"I do have some tricks up my sleeve." He helped her into the truck and went around the front to his door. When he got in, she'd slid across the seat and tucked her hand into his.

"She's going to like me, right?"

"You've already met her." He tossed her a look that said he knew she'd met up with his mother after his disastrous proposal.

"That was just—" She cut her voice into silence. "I was worried about you."

"Then why are you worried about this?"

Belle lifted one shoulder into a shrug. "I don't know. Let's just go."

"I can't shift the truck with you holdin' my hand like that."

"Jace." She peered up at him, letting all her fears and worries out.

He pressed a careful kiss to her lips so as not to ruin them. "Of course she's going to like you. In fact, she wonders how I got someone like you to go out with me." He freed his hand and shifted into reverse. "Heck, I wonder about that all the time."

Belle leaned against him on the drive over to the bistro. "I have something else I want to talk with you about," he said.

"Oh, yeah?"

"It's kind of serious, so we can wait if you want."

"I already feel like I have a nest of snakes in my stomach. Can't be worse than that."

"Are you really that nervous?"

"They're your parents."

"So what? You won't have to live with them or anything." He glanced at her, open curiosity on his face.

"I want them to like me." She couldn't explain why. Jace didn't seem like the type of man who would care if his mom didn't like his girlfriend.

"And they will." He took her hand and kissed her knuckles.

She tried to relax, but all she could do was swallow and that didn't really help at all. "So what did you want to talk about?"

"Kids," he said. "A family."

"Okay, yeah, that's a pretty serious conversation." Her

mind spun with a fresh set of worries. Would they disagree about this too?

"Do you want a family?" He squeezed her hand and laid their joined fingers on her leg.

"Yes," she said.

"Big or small?"

"Whatever the Lord will give us."

He yanked the truck to the right, onto the shoulder, and braked.

"Jace!" Belle braced herself as her adrenaline spiked.

He turned toward her. "You just…you want…." His jaw worked and his eyes blazed with heat.

"What is wrong with you?" she asked. "Why'd you nearly kill us by driving off the road?" She searched his face for an explanation, but all she could find was humility and complete adoration. "I don't understand," she said. "What did I say?"

"You said you wanted to have a family *with me*." His voice came out husky and hollow.

Comprehension dawned on her and Belle leaned into him. "Of course I want to have a family with you. How many cowboys do you think I'm dating?"

He lifted one shoulder and continued to work to contain his emotion.

She focused her attention out the windshield. "You want to know why I slept until almost noon today?"

"If you want to tell me."

"Because I was up until the wee hours of the morning designing my wedding dress." She turned back to him, feeling the seriousness and fire ignite in her bloodstream and her eyes. "The one I'm going to wear when we get married."

"What's it look like?"

"Wouldn't you like to know?" She cupped his face in her palm and stroked her thumb over his lips. "You'll have to decide if you want to marry me first."

"Belle, I want—"

"Don't." She glared at him. "Don't say it unless you really mean it."

"I want...you know, I think I do *want a sandwich for dinner tonight.*" He smirked at her and flipped the truck back into drive.

"You think you're so charming." She nudged him with her shoulder and folded her arms.

"But that's comin', Belle."

"What? A proposal?"

"Yeah, that's happening."

"When?"

"Wouldn't you like to know?"

———

"She's fantastic." Jace's mother almost deafened him with her version of hello.

"She's right here, Mom. She probably heard that." He glanced down to where Belle laid in his lap. She glanced up at him, a drowsy edge in her eyes. Maybe she hadn't heard. She hadn't stirred when he fished his phone from his pocket to answer his mother's call.

"I can see why you love her," his mom continued as if Jace hadn't even spoken. Dinner had ended an hour ago, and Jace knew his mom would call before she went to bed.

"She's pretty amazing," Jace agreed, stroking his fingers up Belle's arm and back to her wrist. "I'm glad you like her."

That got her attention and she stiffened. He shook his head and smiled, which allowed Belle to relax back into his lap. They'd been cuddling on the couch, chatting until he felt chatted out. She'd turned on a movie and promptly fallen asleep, her usual behavior with movies. Just like he ordered a sandwich everywhere they went, she couldn't make it through a movie without a nap.

He let his mom talk for a few minutes, then he said good-bye and hung up. "I should go, Belle." He stroked her hair and jostled her shoulder. "It's late."

She pushed herself to a seated position beside him. "Okay. Sorry I fell asleep." She shot him a sheepish look.

"No, you're not." He chuckled. "I don't mind. I like it when you sleep next to me. It's peaceful."

She smiled drowsily and pressed a kiss to his lips. Hers felt full and soft, and he took his time enjoying them. "See you later." He extracted himself from her arms and stood.

She watched him from the couch as he pulled on his cowboy boots and checked to make sure he had his wallet. "Church tomorrow? Come pick me up?"

"Sure thing, sunshine."

Jace stewed over how he could propose to Belle during the thirty-minute drive back to the ranch, during the entire church service the next day, while they ate side-by-side at the waterfall. Now that he'd said he was going to propose, it seemed to be all he could focus on.

A twinge of fear crept into his head as he dropped her off at her house on Sunday afternoon. *Are you ready to be engaged again?*

As he backed out of her driveway and set his truck on the road, Jace wasn't one-hundred percent sure. He knew he loved Belle. Dr. Fletcher said he'd made great progress. He'd booked several more weeks of equine therapy with Owen.

Jace rolled down his window and took a deep drag of Montana summer air. He felt better than he had in so long, he wasn't sure if this was his new normal or not. Either way, he liked the way he admired the clear blue sky instead of being angry it hadn't rained in a while.

Am I ready, Lord?

Jace rounded the bend in the road, and the waterfalls came into view. And he knew.

Yes, he was ready.

———

Weeks passed, and Jace didn't ask Belle to marry him. He asked her to show him her wedding dress sketches, and he enjoyed the flush that rose to her cheeks and the furious fire that rode in her eyes. She called him a tease and impossible and once, downright mean, but he'd spoken true.

The proposal was coming.

Today, in fact.

Mari started school today, and Rose and Tom were both driving her into town. Jace had noticed a marked difference in both Tom and Rose since they'd been doing the equine therapy. He felt it in himself.

He finished loading the picnic basket, blankets, and the ring he'd chosen for Belle in the back of their SUV. He reached up and pushed the button to close the liftgate.

"Got it all?" Tom appeared at the back of the car.

"Yep."

"We'll get it all set out at the waterfalls."

"We won't be there until noon." Jace swallowed down his rising panic. "That's if Owen can get Belle to go with him." He swiped his hat off his head and wiped a hand through his hair. "I have no idea how he's going to do that."

"Owen has a plan. He'll get her there."

Jace nodded, his mouth set with determination. "Okay, I have to go get some work done." He strode back to the lodge, and he managed to lose himself in normal ranch chores until he needed to leave.

"You leavin'?" Landon pushed through the door right when Jace was going out.

He grinned. "I'm askin' your sister to marry me today."

Landon stared, reminding Jace that he'd never asked Landon about his sudden disinterest in women. Finally, Landon smiled. "I'll hold everything down here."

Jace clapped his friend on the shoulder and left. He didn't drive too fast, or too slow. Timing was everything today, and he couldn't communicate with Owen too much.

He'd planned the proposal down to the minute. It was time to execute it.

———

Belle rode on the second bench of a Silver Creek van as a dark-skinned woman named Norah navigated it across town. Owen had told her about a possible remodel at the facility, and Belle had come to find out more about it. The director of Silver Creek, Dr. Richards, had shown her the girls' dormitories and introduced her to Norah, his "best counselor." Norah had worked at Silver Creek for years, and she knew exactly what the girls needed in their rooms.

She also knew how to get around Gold Valley's narrow streets in a twelve-passenger van. Owen rode in the front, more than happy to have a reason to escape the stables for a few hours. She'd smiled at him when he'd suggested lunch—just the three of them—at the falls. Norah had run off to the kitchen for food, and Belle's stomach grumbled for the want of it.

Norah pulled into the parking lot, and Belle noticed that the park and trails didn't host as many people. "Looks pretty empty," she said. "Seems odd. It's a beautiful day."

"First day of school," Owen said. "Families are gettin' back to their normal schedule." He pulled the bag of food from the back and helped Belle down. She'd taken a few steps when his phone beeped. At the same time, the radio in the van squealed.

Belle waited while he read his phone, while Norah

picked up the radio and began speaking into it. The falls called to her, and she took several steps away to enjoy their joyful noise and experience the playful breeze.

Behind her, the van started. She spun to find it backing out. Owen leaned out of the passenger window. "We have an emergency at the facility. We'll be back in an hour." Norah peeled off before Belle could comprehend his words.

She stared after the white van, her heart leaping and bounding against her throat. They'd left her. Just driven off and left her.

Pure panic paraded through her when she realized she'd left her purse in the van. Her purse, which also contained her phone.

The breeze tugged against her hair, and now it felt like a hurricane-strength gale. She shivered and glanced around the near-empty parking lot. Only a few cars loitered nearest to the trailhead. She took a breath and forced reason into her thoughts.

She was fine. It was a beautiful day without a cloud in sight. She could walk the trail, enjoy the ducks in the pond, maybe even see some wildlife near the higher, hidden pool she and Jace had hiked to several times.

He dominated her thoughts as she started down the boardwalk, which quickly turned into the trail that led around the pools on the other side of the falls. She walked quickly, enjoying the warm air and time to herself.

She turned up the path that led to the upper pools, suddenly quite content to spend some time here alone.

Dismay shot through her when she found someone already in the small meadow preceding the pools.

As she neared, the shape of a cowboy hat formed. A cowboy hat she knew all too well....

"Jace?"

The man stood and came toward her. It *was* Jace. "What are you doing here?"

He swept her into his arms and off her feet. "Waitin' for you."

He set her on her feet and kissed her. "Come on. I have lunch."

Confusion riddled her mind. "*You* have lunch?" Her feet grew roots as she realized she'd been set up. "You had them drive me here and drop me off, didn't you?"

"I wanted it to be a surprise." He tucked his arm around her waist. "And you, Belle Edmunds, are a very hard woman to surprise."

She let him lead her to a denim blanket spread in a patch of sunlight. "What did you get for lunch?"

"Chicken Caesar salad for you." He handed her a lidded bowl he produced from a picnic basket. A picnic basket she'd never seen before. It was almost too Martha Stewart to belong to Jace. "Sandwich and chips for me."

"I like chips too, you know."

He tossed the bag toward her and sat on the blanket across from her. She popped the lid on the salad. "You did not make this."

"Gloria, my boss's wife, did." He pointed toward the basket. "I think there's dressing in there."

Belle stuck a piece of chicken in her mouth and turned her attention to the picnic basket. Instead of finding any dressing, an open jewelry box sat just under the lid. She gasped and choked on the food in her mouth. She managed to swallow as Jace swiped the glittering diamond before she could touch it.

"Belle, I'm in love with you." His eyes twinkled like stars. "I'm ready to take the leap." He looked at the ring and back to her. "Will you marry me?"

He gazed at her with such hope, such love, that both emotions flooded Belle, infused her, lifted her up and into his arms. She laughed with him and kissed him. "Yes," she whispered into the side of his neck. "Yes, I'll marry you."

His fingers stayed steady as he slid the ring on her finger. "It's a white sapphire," he said. "Since your birthday is in September and all. The other piece is studded with diamonds and sort of wraps around like this." He swept his hand toward her thumb, up, and around.

She admired the jewel and beamed at him. "I love it."

"So when can I see that wedding dress?" He slid her a grin.

She gave him a playful shove against his solid shoulder. "About the same time I get to see those diamonds, cowboy."

CHAPTER 23

$\mathcal{B}$elle entered her house and stamped the snow from her boots. "What were we thinking? Getting married in the winter? It's a nightmare." She shed her coat and used one foot to get the boot off the other. "Half the flights are now cancelled, and the weatherman just keeps saying more snow's coming. 'Don't plan to go anywhere for the next two weeks.'" She flopped onto the couch next to Jace, who put his arm around her and drew her in for a kiss.

"It's fine, sunshine. Everyone who needs to be at the wedding is right here."

She looked at him with that blaze that suggested she didn't want his solutions, just his sympathy.

"Your parents are back," he forged on anyway. "Mine are here. Tom's here. Landon too. So who, exactly, are you worried won't make it to the wedding?" He held up his hand. "Don't say you. You're going to be there, right?"

That got her to smile, and she snuggled into his side. "I'm going to be there."

Jace wasn't really asking, though he had several times over the past five months. After a while, Belle just started telling him that yes, she'd be there.

"Hey, this means we'll have a white Christmas." He pressed a kiss to her forehead.

"We always have a white Christmas." She heaved herself off the couch. "You got the invitations sent?"

"All of 'em."

She puttered around the kitchen, making a pot of coffee and then pre-heating the oven for a pan of frozen lasagna her mother had brought over several weeks ago. Jace watched her, recognizing the stress of her movement.

"Why don't you go sew something?" he suggested. "I'll head back out to the ranch, and we'll see each other tomorrow to sample the caterer's options. Okay?"

She didn't turn toward him, but leaned into the counter and gazed through the window. Gazed through the window at all the snow. Montana seemed to exist under a perpetual storm cloud, and though Jace didn't normally dislike winter, this year had tested his patience already.

"Belle?" He sidled up behind her and wrapped his arms around her. "You okay? You know everything is gonna be okay, right?"

"How?"

"'Cause honestly, sweetheart." He touched his lips to her earlobe. "If it was just you and me and the preacher, I'd be just fine. That's all we need, right? Each other and God's blessing?"

She began to sway and he went with her, matching his breathing to hers.

"Belle?"

"I know." She turned into his chest and buried herself in his arms. "I know I just need you and the preacher. But I want everyone to see my dress too."

Jace chuckled and leaned back. "They will, sunshine. I promise you that."

She looked up at him with teary eyes, her sob morphing into a laugh. "You can't promise me that." She touched her lips to his for half a heartbeat. "But thanks for saying it." She molded her mouth to his this time, and Jace couldn't wait for the next seven days to pass so he could become her husband.

———

Belle stepped into her wedding dress, which took both her mom and Ashley to hold for her. She shimmied into the bodice as Ashley kept a tight grip on all the layers and layers of the skirt. Her mom moved behind her to zip it up. "Belle, this is fabulous."

"Thanks, Mom." Her voice caught and she swallowed the emotion back into place. Her makeup had been professionally done, as had her hair. Parted down the middle, with two wispy braids holding the sides back, her auburn locks fell over her bare shoulders.

"You barely fit into it," her mom said, eyeing Belle's chest.

"I just need that tape." She nodded to the skin adhesive she'd ordered online. "Ashley'll do it." Her friend handed the fistful of ivory fabric to Belle and retrieved the body adhesive that would keep all the proper parts covered during the ceremony.

Her mother tugged the dress over Belle's hips and smoothed it down. The semi-mermaid look flared into ruffle upon ruffle as the skirt expanded to a five-foot circle around her feet. She wore a pair of cardinal red heels, and as her mom handed her a bouquet of poinsettias in shades of red, white, and everything in between, Belle felt complete.

Ashley stepped back and scanned Belle. She reached out and tucked a bit more hair behind the braid on the right side. "Perfect."

"You're ready," her mom said.

"I'm ready," Belle echoed. A grin burst through her body and manifested itself on her face. "Is it time?"

"A few more minutes," Ashley said, moving to the door and poking her head out. She found who she was looking for and closed the door. "Two minutes, Belle." She squealed and rushed toward Belle, careful not to tread on the fabric Belle had sewed for over a month.

"I'm so happy you're getting your cowboy." She leaned over the skirt and hugged Belle.

"Thanks, Ashley." Belle sucked the emotion back again as she hugged her mother and the first inklings of the organ music met her ears.

Ashley opened the door, and Belle stepped to her father's side. "Hey, Daddy."

He gave her a quick kiss on the cheek and offered her his arm. They moved down the hall and took their position behind the closed doors of the chapel. She took a deep breath, her heart battering her ribcage and her nerves tap dancing against her bones.

"Ready, sweetheart?"

She nodded, ready to see Jace, inhale Jace, kiss Jace, become Jace's wife forever. "Ready."

Her father knocked once and the door swung in to reveal a crowd gathered in the pews. The world narrowed to just the man standing at the end of the aisle. He wore a suit and vest the color of charcoal, with a delicate white poinsettia pinned to his lapel. His tie matched her heels and the deepest red poinsettias in her bouquet.

She couldn't stop smiling. Jace watched her slow progress toward him with that dangerous, devilish glint in his eye, barely noticeable from beneath his brand new dark gray cowboy hat.

Her father passed her to Jace, who leaned in and whispered, "You take my breath away every time I see you."

Her nerves wouldn't allow her to respond vocally, but she lifted her arm and ran her fingers along the brim of his hat.

"Thank you for showin' up." He kicked a grin at her, and she returned it.

The pastor started speaking, and she faced him, the solid weight of Jace's arm against her side grounding her and comforting her. She listened, but the words she'd written for her vows seemed to rush from the pastor's mouth. Jace's were read, and while Belle knew she wouldn't be able to remember them, she clung to the feeling of peace, of safety, of love she felt from the man next to her.

He'd always adored her, and he'd shown her that he treasured her often over the past several months of their engagement.

"Do you, Belle Mae Edmunds, take Jace Leland Lovell to be your lawfully wedded husband, in sickness and in health, for better or for worse, for richer or for poorer, to love and to cherish until death parts you?"

She couldn't look away from Jace, whose jaw worked against his emotions. "Yes."

The pastor started the question for Jace, who lost the battle against his tears. He swiped quickly at his face and smiled.

"Yes." With his spoken vow, she leaned over and kissed him, taking her time to enjoy and commit to memory her first kiss with her husband.

———

Read on for the first couple of chapters of the next book in the Horseshoe Home Ranch Romance series, **SNOWED IN WITH THE COWBOY!**

SNEAK PEEK! SNOWED IN WITH THE COWBOY CHAPTER ONE

*T*he announcer's voice reverberated through Sterling Maughan's head, bringing him away from the edge of unconsciousness and back to the X-Games blaring from the TV.

He knew that voice. Hated that voice, especially after it had broken up with him on live, national television.

He fumbled for the remote so he could change the channel, the pain in his leg amping up to a sharp ache. One glance at the clock on the Blu-ray player told him he'd missed his last dosage of painkillers by an hour.

Sterling didn't care. When the nurse came, she'd force-feed it to him. He hit a button and that traitorous, cheating female voice changed into the theme song for a cooking show. He lowered the volume and dropped the remote. It made a weird clunking sound as it hit last night's pizza box. Or maybe last week's pizza box. Sterling had stopped cleaning up after his first night at the cabin, eight days ago.

Sleep eluded him for a few minutes as he listened to the evening wind batter the windows. At least it wasn't the neighbors—the closest ones up here in Gold Valley's exclusive cabin community were at least a hundred yards away.

Not that Sterling had been admiring the lush pine forest and miles of trails surrounding his family's cabin. He hadn't moved from the couch in the basement for more than the necessities for days. His eyes drifted closed and despite the pain in his leg, he sank into the darkness that had consumed his mind so readily since the accident.

A thump from the second floor jolted him awake. His heart pounded as his mind frantically searched for an explanation to the sound. The wind had died, but it could've been an animal. Could've been a raccoon or a rat.

A scrape echoed through the ceiling, like someone—not a raccoon or a rat—had slid a chair across the floor. Sterling sat up, fully awake now.

Because someone was in the house.

He calmed his breathing and swallowed his pulse back to its proper spot in his chest. His police training required him to be alert, focused, and calm in stressful situations. True, he hadn't been active in his unit since last fall, when he'd started the professional snowboarding circuit. But once a cop, always a cop.

He stood, careful to put minimal weight on his still-healing knee. The cast had come off last week, but he still wore a full leg brace, which made walking difficult. And climbing stairs? Sterling hadn't done it in weeks.

His back creaked with his first step, and his left foot felt numb because of the reduced circulation from the brace. A pain behind his right eye balanced both sides of his body with aches he couldn't erase with a couple of pills.

Another noise—bump, ba-bump—from the second floor urged him toward the stairs, where he lifted his good leg first. One down, fifteen to go.

For the first time, he cursed the size of the cabin—which was a ridiculous name for it. It was a mansion, a luxury lodge. Seven thousand square feet, spanning three floors. Two kitchens, one on the main level where the noise came from, one in the basement where he was living. Ten bathrooms. Eight bedrooms. A game room, a library, and two living rooms.

Definitely a luxury lodge. But the people in the gated resort community called them cabins, so Sterling did too.

His father had done very well in the real estate business, as his mother liked to point out to Sterling about every third month. He'd never been a conformist, and it showed as all five of his older brothers had gone on to law school at William & Mary, or medical school at Johns Hopkins, or banking and finance at Stanford.

Sterling had graduated in the middle of his class from the Police Academy in Salt Lake City.

Still, he steadily climbed the stairs, his good foot planted before lifting that blasted left leg. His mind wandered through a list of who could possibly be at the cabin. His parents had gone to Madagascar for a university internship in January and certainly wouldn't return only three months into the eight-month program.

His brothers all had a key to the cabin, but everyone but Rex lived in other states. Rex lived in Missoula, an hour and a half away, running their father's real estate firm, and he hadn't mentioned coming up to the cabin.

Sterling's fingers fisted, almost hoping for a fight. At least he knew the police officer in him hadn't been snuffed out. He didn't know if he'd be able to return to the force, what with his injuries and all, but he felt confident in his abilities to incapacitate—

—A curvy woman.

Sterling stalled at the top of the stairs and stared at the African-American woman standing in the kitchen, leaning over something he couldn't see. She wore a tight pair of jeans and a long-sleeved shirt—not exactly burglary clothing.

Women can be killers too, he thought just before the loudest music he'd ever heard blasted through the house.

The woman shook her booty to the music as she pulled on a pair of yellow rubber gloves. Sterling stared, wondering if she'd put on the rap to cover the sound of his screams and the gloves to prevent the possibility of leaving fingerprints. He couldn't decide if he should dial 911 or laugh at her terrible dance moves.

A smile formed on his face—possibly the first since his fall eleven weeks ago. He suddenly became aware that he hadn't showered or shaved in many days, and fought the urge to rush downstairs and attend to his personal hygiene needs.

As he scrubbed his fingers along his scruffy beard, the

woman spun around, her eyes half open. Open enough to catch on his though, and she stopped short. Her gloved hand came to her mouth—gross, Sterling thought—and her chocolaty eyes widened.

He lifted his hand in greeting, his smile reducing itself by half. She spun and fumbled at the source of the hip-hop beat, finally silencing it. She placed one hand over her heart as her chest rose and fell, rose and fell. "You scared me."

Sterling leaned against the wall to give some relief to his aching leg, but otherwise held his position. "What's up?"

"Nothing." The woman gestured to a bucket of cleaning supplies at her feet. "I'm here to clean the cabin." She glanced around like someone would appear to corroborate her story, her black curls swinging from side to side. "I didn't know anyone would be here."

Sterling's gaze swept the counter behind her, focusing on several bags of groceries. "Are you staying?"

"Yes." She followed his gaze to the fruit and bread. "I'm bringing my girls up here tonight."

"Girls?" Confusion clouded Sterling's mind, his words. "What girls?"

"I work at the teen rehabilitation center at the base of the mountain," she explained. "You know, Silver Creek, the one with the horses?"

Sterling had been coming to his family's cabin his entire life. He'd never heard of a teen rehabilitation center. "No, I have no idea about Silver Creek or the horses."

"Oh, well, I work there." The woman spoke with her hands, and Sterling worried about the germs spewing from those gloves, though they were probably cleaner than he was. She seemed to realize how ridiculous she looked with those toilet gloves on, because she stripped them off as a dark red stained her cheeks.

"It's a rehabilitation program for teens with addictions," she continued. "They live on-site for ninety days, and part of their therapy is to learn to work with horses as they overcome their problems. I'm a counselor." She took a deep breath, probably because she hadn't done so once since she started talking.

Sterling cocked one eyebrow at the speed with which she delivered her spiel. "And?"

"And I clean your family's cabin. I've been doing it for a few years."

"And you bring your girls up here?"

"When they reach the halfway point of their stay, they get to go on an outing if they've followed the rules and stayed clean. Your mom has given me permission to bring them to Six Sons. We'll be here for three days."

Oh, no they wouldn't. Sterling had some very important recovering to do. Alone. No teen addicts. No beautiful, exotic camp counselors. Just pizza and cooking shows and sleeping while the drugs kept the pain at bay.

"You're Sterling Maughan," the woman said.

Sterling felt the weight of her proclamation, spoken in a tone of awe and reverence like he was worthy of such things. "Yeah."

She blinked a couple of times, and Sterling could practically hear the words she wanted to say before she said them.

Terrible about what that Amber Lyons did to you. And on national TV too.

He braced himself as she opened her mouth. "I'm Norah Watson." Her eyes scanned his height, coming back to his face a moment later. "I'm sorry about your fall. Will you ever snowboard again?"

Ah, wasn't that the question of the year? Sterling didn't know the answer, so he lifted one shoulder in a half-shrug. Emotion surged up his throat, along with the feel of the wind against his face, the smell of a fresh snowfall, where it stuck no matter how hard he tried to swallow it back.

"I've seen you race," she said. "You were like liquid on the mountain. So smooth."

"Thanks," he managed to croak. He actually would've preferred she gave him her condolences about his ex-girl-friend. He'd at least be able to find another date someday. But snowboarding had always come before women, and he couldn't articulate yet how much he'd lost when he'd lost snowboarding.

"You can't stay here," he said, his rough voice matching the shredded edges in his chest.

Panic crossed her face, troubling her lips and causing a twitch in her fingers. "But I have to. The girls have been working so hard for this outing."

Unrest swirled in his gut. "I'm staying here for a while." How long, he didn't know. He didn't have anything else to do, and nowhere else to go, and no one to see.

Norah began unpacking the groceries. "How about we strike a deal?"

"A deal?" Sterling folded his arms and watched her work.

"You're obviously living downstairs." She tossed him a look over her shoulder that said, Right?

He didn't indicate an answer either way, just waited for her to continue.

"This place is three levels. We always stay upstairs in the bunk bed room." She glanced to the ceiling like she could see the bunk beds from here. "I have eight girls in my group, and you won't even know we're here. We'll stay on the top two levels. There's a kitchen here, and one downstairs for you." She gave him another up-down glance. "You're obviously not going to be traipsing around the property, and we'll be gone before you even know we're here."

He doubted it. He'd heard her, and he'd been half-asleep. What would eight teenage girls sound like?

Chickens, he thought. Or elephants.

"I have to turn in a strict itinerary for these outings." She reached for a binder on the counter. "You can see our schedule if you want. We'll be gone cross-country skiing most of the morning tomorrow, and I only let them go down to the game room once, on Saturday evening, and we'll be back in bed by ten both nights. I promise."

She lifted a paper toward him, but Sterling waved it away. Though the game room took up considerable space on the bottom level, where he was living, he hadn't used it since he'd arrived, and he wasn't planning to. It also had a separate entrance, around the side of the garage. He barely used the kitchen in the basement, opting to pick up his cell phone and order, well, pizza. Everything was easier than trying to explain where the front door really was, and the sidewalk leading around the side of the house from the driveway led to a door he didn't have to climb any stairs to answer, which was why living on the bottom level had been his first choice when he'd come to the cabin several weeks ago.

"I don't want a bunch of girls here," he said.

"But you won't even know we're here."

"I knew you were here." He gave her a pointed look. "And I have my home health nurses coming twice a day. That can't be disrupted."

"Of course not. And I won't blast any rap music." She crossed her heart. "Only Mozart. Soothing. I promise." Her lips tugged upward, and something slipped in Sterling's resolve.

"I don't know...the doctor said I need a lot of rest." He glanced out the windows located above the spiral staircase that led downstairs. "My mom didn't say anything about this when I told her I was coming here."

Norah smiled like she'd won. "Well, I'll call Nancy right now and ask her."

When she mentioned his mom, Sterling felt the victory blow land against his lungs. The last thing he wanted was to talk to her, especially after their last conversation.

"Don't do that," he said. "I guess I can put up with you for three days."

———

Norah put away the rest of the groceries under the misses-nothing eye of Sterling Maughan. The Sterling Maughan. The one who'd won gold at the last Olympics and had been set to sweep every event in this winter's X-Games.

Of course, that was before the Break-Up to End All Break-Ups, and then the devastating fall that had broken his left femur and cracked part of his pelvis.

He looked good for such an injury, standing there glowering at her, wearing a T-shirt that pulled across his broad shoulders, a loose pair of gym shorts, and the bulkiest leg brace she'd ever seen. At least he could stand, and he certainly hadn't lost his brooding good looks in the accident. Norah had seen enough interviews to know.

"Do you need help getting down the stairs?" She didn't turn to look at him as she asked. Someone with as many muscles as Sterling could snap her in half with his bare hands. He didn't look as though he'd lost anything in the bicep department since his accident.

His dark eyes didn't dance the way they had on the medal podium, though. And while she'd seen him in countless family photos—always alone, surrounded by his five older brothers and their wives and families—she hadn't realized how dark his hair was. The colors on her old TV were obviously lacking.

"I could use some help, yes."

His words surprised her, but she crossed through the kitchen and stepped down the two stairs to the living room. This particular staircase that led to the basement spiraled, and she knew from experience that going down was harder than going up. Especially because the last three stairs were very steep and quite uneven.

"I'll go first," she said. "You can brace your weight on my shoulders." She moved down a few steps and stopped. The heat of his hands on her shoulders sent a shiver through her she hoped he didn't notice.

Giddiness swept through her. Her half-brother would never believe she'd met Sterling Maughan, the professional athlete that was pure celebrity for the people in Gold Valley. As they moved painstakingly down the steps, Norah toyed with the idea of asking him for a picture. Would she come off as a gushing fan? A lunatic? Some flirty girl? Utterly insensitive?

When they reached the bottom floor, Norah gasped at the sight of the living room. A nest—a real, live, human-sized nest!—on the couch showed where Sterling had obviously been living. Soda cans, pizza boxes, paper wrappers, straws, and clothes littered the floor in a six-foot radius from the nest.

"How long have you been here?" she asked, taking in the unlit fireplace, the TV, glowing with instructions on how to grill ribs, above the mantle. He obviously hadn't used any of the three bedrooms down here. The door to the closest bathroom stood open, but all the blinds on the wall of windows that would normally show a deck and breath-taking winter scenery had been tightly shut.

"Since last week." Sterling hobbled into the kitchen— much smaller than the one on the main floor, but certainly sufficient for this bachelor sixth son.

She followed him, freezing as he downed a handful of pills. Just the sound the caplets made against the plastic bottle conjured old hurts and images she'd rather forget. She forced her feet to move and reached under the sink for a garbage bag. Fluffing it open, she began to fill it with a week's worth of fast food waste.

"You don't have to do that," Sterling said.

"It's my job." Norah winced as she caught a whiff of Sterling's socks. "Your mom pays me to do this."

Sterling made a grab for a pair of discarded board shorts, and Norah pulled back. "I don't need you to do my laundry."

"I don't do laundry."

"Great."

"But I'm killer at picking up trash." She gave him a wide berth as she moved around the couch and reached for the pizza box. The remote fell off, and she put it on the coffee table.

"I can do it." But Sterling sank back into his nest and lifted his injured leg with his hands. He groaned as he placed it on the stack of pillows he'd laid out on the coffee table.

Watching him, a flash of what life would be like if Norah had a lot of money stole through her head. Yes, the sports news feeds had been full of Poor Sterling Maughan. His career is over just as it was picking up momentum. And too bad about his girlfriend being such a cheater….

But "poor Sterling Maughan" was anything but poor.

He wasn't working two jobs and going to school at night

just to pay the electric bill and put food on the table and make sure his mama had the medicine she needed. Norah tasted the bitterness of her situation on the back of her tongue, and it was too familiar. She hated feeling this way, and yet she couldn't push down the negative vibes.

She stuck a smile on her face as she tied the now-full trash bag. "Hey, can I ask a huge favor? My half-brother is a big fan of yours. Could I get a picture with you?"

Sterling looked up, his eyes half glazed from the pills. Strong jealousy Norah hadn't felt in a while surged through her. She managed to push it away.

"Sure, I guess." The disinterest in his voice didn't fall on deaf ears, but Norah whipped her phone from her back pocket anyway. She wanted to spray an entire can of disinfectant on his nest before she sat down, but she flopped down on the blanket at his side like it was a throne fit for a queen. A puff of foul-smelling air surrounded them, but Norah contained a cringe.

"Okay, smile." She focused on the two of them, but Sterling's smile looked more like a grimace. Maybe she'd jostled his leg too much. Something whispered inside her that it wasn't just his leg giving him trouble.

Norah snapped the picture and turned toward Sterling. They sat close enough for her breath to brush his cheek. He kept his mouth steadfastly shut, and if she had to guess, she should be happy she couldn't smell his breath.

As she watched him, she felt his sadness penetrate her defenses. Felt his helplessness. Her mother had always told her she had a compassionate heart and was able to sense someone in distress, which was why she'd been taking classes in social work for the past year.

"I'm sorry," she whispered, unable to break eye contact with the damaged once-pro-snowboarder.

He blinked, shrugged, laid his head back, closed his eyes. "It happens."

Norah stood, haunted by the finality in his tone.

Help him, she prayed, unable to do much more than that for the man who wore his emotional turmoil so openly. As she went back upstairs to finish preparations for her girls, she promised herself she'd check in on Sterling over the next couple of days. Even though he had nurses coming, he seemed like he could use a friend.

SNEAK PEEK! SNOWED IN WITH THE COWBOY CHAPTER TWO

*N*orah maneuvered down the mountain from Six Sons Cabin, careful to stay near the center of the road. March had been brutal in the weather department, and the merrily shining sun only lent light, not warmth. Certainly not enough heat to melt the snow and ice this high above sea level.

She checked the clock on the dashboard and eased up on the brakes. She needed to return to Silver Creek before two o'clock so she could take her girls to their weekly riding session. After that, they usually went to dinner in the cafeteria, but tonight, they'd load into a Silver Creek van and head up to the cabin. She was glad, because the cafeteria was currently under construction in preparation for a complete makeover.

Norah was planning a cookout and had quickly swept the snow off the second-level deck before leaving Sterling to his painkillers and cooking shows. The image of his sunken eyes pulled at her heart. On TV, he'd always been full of life and quick to pump his fist after a successful run. The man she'd met had become a shell of the one she'd seen on TV, a ghost of who she saw in the pictures scattered around the cabin.

You need to help him. The thought entered her mind unbidden, and Norah felt its power. Her fingers tightened on the wheel as she rounded the last bend in the road before it straightened out and dipped into the valley.

"How?" she asked herself. She had no idea how to deal with an injury like Sterling's, though she did understand why people smoked, or drank, or turned to cutting. Having experienced similar home conditions as the girls she worked with, she'd dealt with her share of problems and temptations.

The pull to escape her life just for an hour threaded through her. A single painkiller would give her those sixty minutes.

The constant emotional effort she had to expend to take care of her mama sometimes weighed Norah down to the point where she couldn't get out of bed until she psyched herself up.

Normal twenty-seven-year-olds didn't care for their half-brothers full time, play nursemaid to a woman who should be able to take care of herself, or mother eight troubled teens. As Norah turned a corner, she wanted the life that single women her age enjoyed. And with that yearning came a punch of guilt that hit her right in the lungs.

She pushed away the tide of bitter feelings. Her three

half-brothers depended on Norah for everything, and with their mama sick, Norah certainly couldn't add another invalid to her plate. And yet, she felt a strong attraction to Sterling that went beyond his celebrity status.

She parked in the staff lot and leapt from her car, determined to think about Sterling later. As she stopped by the administration office to turn in the girls' permission slips, she found Dr. Richards dictating a job notice to his secretary.

Norah listened as she flipped through the pages she already knew were in order. When Dr. Richards finished, Norah handed him the papers. "We're headed up to Six Sons tonight. We'll be back on Monday in time for dinner."

Dr. Richards didn't look at the permission paperwork. "Sounds good, Norah. I want you to pay particular attention to Genn while you're up there. She had a hard session this morning."

Norah nodded and swung her chin toward the secretary. "You need a new counselor?"

Dr. Richards handed the paperwork to his secretary and stepped into his office, a sigh filled with exhaustion escaping his lips. "Yes, Will quit today. He's staying on until the end of this cycle." He settled at his desk and pulled a file toward him. "I know you'd take on another group, but I need a male."

"I might know someone." Norah spoke before she could think. Or maybe Sterling had never really left her mind.

"Oh?" Dr. Richards glanced up and held her gaze. "Who? What experience does he have?"

"Well, he probably doesn't have any." Norah twisted her fingers around themselves. Why had she spoken?

"Is he over twenty-five?"

"Yes." Norah had seen Sterling snowboard countless times, had watched a couple of interviews on ESPN, and knew he was twenty-six.

"He's not employed?"

Norah thought of Sterling's nest, the greasy texture of his hair, the length of that beard, the smell of his dirty socks. "He...he used to be a cop. But he got hurt."

Dr. Richards perked up. "A cop? Maybe he could work with our at-risk group."

The at-risk boys that came to Silver Creek often had violent histories, usually involving weapons rather than drugs.

"Maybe," Norah said.

"Get an application from Shelly," Dr. Richards said. "See if he wants to apply."

Norah said good-bye and stepped into the outer office to get an application for Sterling. With the single sheet of paper in her hand, she felt like she had something concrete to do for him.

Ten minutes later, she stood at the end of the hall on the second floor of the girls' building. "Team Silver Bow!" she called. The four doors nearest her opened within a few seconds of each other and her eight girls entered the hall.

They each wore the required horseback attire: long pants, long-sleeved shirts, and boots. They carried coats and hats and gloves. Norah smiled at each girl, noticing that

Genn's eyes stayed on the floor, and her roommate, Hailey, seemed to have been crying.

Though her motherly instincts kicked in, Norah kept quiet. It wasn't her job to provide therapy. She was there to facilitate their schedules, get them to meals on time, establish the rules, and be a listening ear should the girls choose to tell her something. Nothing the girls told her was private, and Norah hated that, but it kept her out of difficult situations.

"You ready to ride?" she asked.

Varying responses came from the girls, ranging from mild interest to sarcasm to genuine enthusiasm. Norah stepped to the head of the line and led them downstairs and around the building. As they entered the March wind, Norah sucked in a breath and prayed for an early spring.

"Just think, ladies," she said over her shoulder. "In just a couple of hours, we'll be sitting by a huge fireplace, sipping hot chocolate."

Natalie, a bubbly fourteen-year-old, cheered from behind her. "Can I ride Kimchi today?"

"You ride who you're given," Norah said. "But I'll try to line you up with her."

The girls entered the barn, where Silver Creek's wrangler had eight horses already in stalls. He came out of the tack room, saw the girls, and adjusted his white cowboy hat. "Afternoon, ladies."

One of the girls giggled, and Norah sent a glare down the line. The strict non-fraternizing rules sometimes wore on the girls, especially the flirtier ones. They hadn't seen or spoken to a boy in six weeks, besides Dr. Richards and Owen, the horseman now smiling down on them in all his Montana cowboy glory.

He pointed to the horses behind him. "We got a new gelding this mornin'. His name's Pompeii. Who wants to ride 'im first?" Owen's gaze swept the girls, his keen eyes searching for something Norah didn't understand.

"Genn?" Owen asked, leaving Norah to wonder if Owen could read more than horses.

"Sure." Genn stepped over to the unfamiliar dark horse with a black mane and tail.

"Nat," Norah hissed. "Trade places with Felicia."

The two girls switched, and Natalie got assigned to Kimchi, the brown and white paint horse she preferred. Norah stayed in the barn as Owen reminded the girls how to mount the horse and hold the reins. Her chest filled with love as Genn leaned over and patted Pompeii's neck, a smile pulling at the corner of her mouth. Norah had experienced many "hard sessions" during her time at Silver Creek, and as much as she didn't want to, she saw herself in Genn. A good girl, without the resources or support to do much with her life.

But in the six weeks since Genn arrived, Norah had seen strides in her she hadn't experienced herself. Genn's parents had started coming to the group counseling sessions, something Mama had never done for Norah.

Warmth expanded in Norah's chest. Genn would make it. She'd do something great with her life, not be confined to Gold Valley and her childhood home the way Norah was.

Norah wanted nothing but success and happiness for the girl, for all her girls.

For Sterling too, she thought, startled by how easily the man had wormed his way into her mind. She'd spent maybe fifteen minutes with him—which was fifteen more minutes than she'd spent with someone of the opposite sex in quite a long time.

That's why, she told herself as she waited for the girls to return from their ride. Since she still lived at home with her three younger half-brothers—and her sick mama—Norah didn't have time to go on many dates, what with two jobs and a night class. And she wasn't all that interested in growing close to a man only to watch him leave when things got hard.

She'd seen that too many times in Mama's life. Their front door seemed to rotate with men. But when the bills piled too high, or the baby cried too loud, or Mama got too demanding, those men left.

Norah had never left. She couldn't. Especially not now with Mama's lung disease so advanced and so debilitating. The swell of resentment reared again, nearly choking her.

Her phone rang, and she swiped open the call from her half-brother, Javier. "What's up?"

"Hey, Norah. Mama said it's your girls' weekend, but I want to go to the movies with Sarah and Mateo."

Norah smiled at the rush in Javier's voice and waited while he presented his case.

"So I went and got a movie for Alex and Erik, and they're

set with popcorn and hot chocolate. I just wanted to run it by you, make sure it's okay."

A pinch behind Norah's eyes reminded her that she wasn't the only one paying the price for Mama's illnesses. "Do you have enough money for the movies?"

"Yeah. Anthony paid me this morning." Javier worked for the Mexican grocer as much as possible, but Norah could never take his money, even if she sometimes needed it. A senior in high school, Javier would have to make his own ends meet soon enough.

"Okay. Who's driving?"

"Mateo."

Norah nodded though Javier couldn't see her. Sarah had slid into a snow bank last winter, and Norah felt safer with Mateo driving. "Sounds like you've got it worked out."

"I do, Norah. Thanks."

She hung up, glad for her girls' weekend. She needed the time away from Mama's depression, her medication schedule, her pessimism. Sometimes Norah wondered if she babied her mother too much, but she wasn't sure how not to. She'd been forced to act as mother way before she should've, and a sticky film coated her mouth as she tried to swallow back the trapped feelings. They came every so often, and Norah couldn't help wondering if her mind was as messed up as Mama's.

To prove she wasn't a slave to her demons, Norah poured everything she had into taking care of her girls. At least with them, she could witness growth and change and healing—something she'd never see in her mama. Sadness filled her, and her soul ached for a solution to her mother's mental and physical challenges. She wanted to help, she just didn't know how.

Again, Sterling's handsome face filled her mind, and a smidgeon of annoyance sang through her.

———

Sterling heard the girls enter the cabin shortly after five o'clock. He'd just come out of the bathroom, where he'd showered and shaved for the first time in several days. It had been as hard as he'd anticipated, even with the shower bench that provided some relief for his leg. Simply getting the brace off had taken him five minutes.

Frustration flooded him as he considered the brace. He really didn't want to put it back on, but he felt the weakness in his leg without it. He didn't want his recovery to take longer than necessary, but reasoned that a few more minutes without the brace wouldn't set him back that much.

He picked up his phone—no messages, no calls—and almost slammed it back onto the kitchen counter. Before the accident, he hadn't been able to keep up with the number of people wanting to talk to him. Family and friends. Those who wanted to be friends. People who wanted an interview, or to talk about a sponsorship, or to film his practice session.

Gratitude filled him that no cameras or reporters had been at the practice session when he'd fallen. The last thing he needed was to watch that horror over and over again on the Internet.

"Sterling?" Norah's voice bounced down the steps. Her body followed a few seconds later, screeching to a halt when she found him leaning against the kitchen counter. Her eyes brightened, slid down the length of his body. When they returned to his again, he saw the same look he'd seen in other girls' eyes. Appreciation. Maybe something a bit warmer.

"You're up." Her voice sounded flirtier, and Sterling couldn't help the zing of satisfaction spiraling through him. He'd been desirable once. Even though his phone sat silent, here was a woman looking at him as if she liked what she saw. That had to count for something.

She grinned at him, and he found himself returning it, thinking maybe *she* could be his friend. "You shaved."

Sterling rubbed his hands along his jaw. "Yeah, it was time." His gaze lingered on her curly hair and sparkling eyes, his face heating when he realized *he* liked what he saw too.

"I'm making hamburgers and hot dogs for the girls." She hooked her thumb over her shoulder toward the stairs. "You want one?"

Sterling's stomach grumbled. "Sure."

"Which? Hamburger or hot dog?"

"Yes," Sterling said, and Norah laughed.

"Okay, both. It'll be a few minutes."

"Take your time." Sterling watched her head back up the stairs before he allowed himself to scan the living room. His clothes still lay scattered around and the room seemed too dark.

He limped over to the window and opened the blinds that faced north, but they let in very little light now that the sun had started to go down. Still, with the view of snow-covered pines and a dusky sky, new life entered his body.

He bent to pick up his clothes. After one trip to the laundry room, Sterling's leg throbbed in protest. He took the time to strap on the brace before he finished tidying up.

Norah returned with two plates filled with a hamburger, a hot dog, coleslaw, potato chips and baby carrots. Embarrassment flooded Sterling's cheeks. "Wow, you think I can eat all that?"

"I have three brothers," she said. "I *know* you can eat all that."

He chuckled as she set the plates on the kitchen counter. "And you even made sure I got vegetables." Sterling slid her a glance, hoping she'd hear the teasing note in his voice. "You make your girls eat all their vegetables?"

She stared at him with a blank face. "Absolutely. Carrots are the building blocks of nutrition for wayward girls."

Sterling settled onto a barstool as he laughed, glad when Norah joined in. "This might be the first meal I haven't eaten on the couch or in bed since my accident."

Norah leaned against the pillar next to the fridge. "Is the burger cooked okay?"

Sterling bit into it, immediately categorizing the meat as overcooked. Charred might be a better description. He forced himself to chew, chew, chew, and swallow. "Delicious." He picked up a bottle of water and downed half of it to get the dry beef to slide down his throat.

Norah seemed to swell under his compliment, and a kernel of interest popped inside Sterling. What kind of person was she? Why did she work with addicted teenagers? How did she come to be cleaning cabins in this exclusive gated community?

"So you don't have any sisters?" Sterling asked, skillfully avoiding taking another bite by engaging in conversation.

"Nope."

"Me either."

"I know," Norah said. "I've been dusting your pictures for years. You were a cute kid." Her smile infected him, and a layer of darkness lifted from his mind.

"Cute." He ate a few potato chips—surely Norah hadn't made those—wondering if anyone would ever find him worth more than *cute*. He could barely put weight on his leg, and the angry, red scars proved he still had a long road ahead of him.

"Anyway, I've got to get back to the girls. I just wanted to let you know that tomorrow we're going cross country skiing in the morning," Norah said. "We have skills in the afternoon, and we'll come down for game night after dinner, but I'll try to keep them as quiet as I can."

"Don't worry about it," Sterling said, ducking his head so he wouldn't have to look at her. "I kinda like having you here. The cabin doesn't feel so…big."

Norah patted his forearm like he was an obedient dog and headed for the stairs. "See you later."

Sterling's skin tingled where she'd touched it, and he trailed his fingers where hers had just been. "Hey, thanks for the food." He watched her wave over her shoulder as she disappeared up the stairs, not quite sure why his stomach squeezed or why he wanted her to stay for a few more minutes. Maybe with his phone so silent, it simply felt good to talk to someone again.

———

By the next evening, Sterling wanted to order pizza again. Norah was not the best of cooks, though she obviously tried hard. But the waffles she served him at breakfast tasted more like salt than anything else, and the soup she'd brought him for lunch was nothing more than water with noodles and overcooked carrots. And the bread? Well, Sterling didn't think *that* was bread.

Sterling took a bite or two before engaging her in whatever conversation he could. She only stayed for a few minutes anyway, as she couldn't leave the girls for long. He'd raided the pantry, eaten all the stale peanut butter crackers his mom kept there, even went so far as to consider making a boxed dinner. He didn't want to hurt Norah's feelings, so he thumbed off his phone and laid it next to him on the couch.

She brought down a pizza box with the girls, ushering them all into the game room while she approached with a literal slice of heaven. "Pizza tonight."

Sterling practically leapt off the couch to get to it.

"Thanks, Norah." He beamed at her, his mouth watering for cheese and pepperoni. "You guys have already eaten?" The box held half a pie.

She giggled, the sound worming past his eardrums and accelerating his heartbeat. "Yeah. That's all yours."

He put his hand on her shoulder, realizing too late the effect that would have on his already fragile emotions. She startled under the weight of his touch, and when their eyes met, something passed between them.

Sterling almost sensed that Norah was as lonely as he was. *Impossible,* he told himself. She had a job surrounded by people. A family who she spent every evening with. Still, with the moments stretching between them, and his stupid hand still on her shoulder, Sterling felt something stir within him.

He cleared his throat and settled his weight away from her. She fell back two steps, her hands sliding up her arms from elbow to shoulder, as if cold. "Okay, well, we'll be down here for a few hours. Hope we don't bother you."

Sterling couldn't quite get his voice to tell her that she certainly didn't bother him. Instead, he lifted a piece of pizza from the box and waved at her. With food in his stomach, he didn't feel so jumpy, but he still wanted to join Norah in the game room and find out everything about her.

Sunday morning, she skipped downstairs to ask him if he wanted to go to church with her and the girls. Sterling hadn't quite known how to answer. His family was religious—the many and varied decorations around the house testified of that. He walked past a picture of Jesus every morning on the way to the bathroom, and a huge glass vase next to the hearth boasted the word "Faith" down the front.

In the end, he'd said no and retreated to his bedroom, where another television and another cooking show held his attention until he heard the girls leave.

Religion was just another way Sterling had rebelled from the perfect, educated, spiritually powerful Maughan family. As he waited for Norah to return, he couldn't help wondering if he would've been spared from the accident had he been more concerned with what God thought about him than what the country thought.

He banished the reminders of Amber, determined not to relive the things she'd said, the way her infidelity had been discovered on live TV because she forgot to remove her mic before meeting up with her secret boyfriend.

Monday, Norah brought down a steaming bowl of spaghetti and a slice of homemade bread for lunch. "Not sure on the bread," she said. "The girls made it—it's part of their treatment. They have to learn new skills to replace their bad habits. Genn made this, and well, she thinks she may have forgotten something."

Sterling eyed the bread, remembering the earlier disaster he'd tasted. Maybe he'd judged Norah prematurely. "Did one of the girls make that bread on Saturday?"

"No, that was my demo loaf. They made theirs today."

Sterling's appetite vanished. If these girls had Norah for a culinary instructor, he didn't hold much hope for this round of bread. "Well, it looks right."

"Well, salt looks like sugar, too." Norah giggled, and Sterling jerked his hand away from the bread.

"You're kidding, right?"

"I honestly don't know." Norah smiled, a warm, happy grin that made Sterling want to figure out if she always felt as joyful as she looked.

"You leaving today?"

"I'm taking the girls back in a few minutes," Norah said. "They have a group therapy session this afternoon. While they're doing that, I'll come back here to clean up."

Sterling's heart pounced against his ribs, for no reason he could name. "I'm probably going to take another nap." He gave her a half-smile, pleased when she rolled her eyes.

"Don't you have physical therapy or something?"

"Yeah," Sterling said. "I do the exercises the doctor told me to." Only for the past three days, but Norah didn't need to know that. "I have to go to Missoula next week for a check-up. Make sure everything's healing right. Whatever." He waved his fork in the air like a magic wand and twirled it in the spaghetti.

Norah put her hand on his shoulder as she stood. He froze, every nerve ending suddenly firing on all cylinders.

She yanked her hand back as if she could feel the increased energy coursing through him. "I hope your recovery continues to go well." She glanced around, her eyes sweeping over surfaces, decorations, and his open bedroom door. "Seems like things have gotten better around here." She spoke like she knew that until she showed up, he hadn't showered in days, hadn't gotten off the couch, hadn't been doing his physical therapy.

"Norah," he said, his voice a tick too thick. "Thank you for this weekend." His stomach might not be so grateful, but his psyche certainly was.

She stared at him, mouth slightly open, those beautiful brown eyes blinking and blinking and blinking. "You're welcome?"

He chuckled, though he wondered why her statement sounded like a question. "I mean it. It's been...nice having you here. So, you know, thanks."

"No problem." She stepped away, and Sterling racked his brain for another topic of conversation. With his mind blank, he flashed her a tight smile and took a bite of the bread—Norah could take lessons from Genn on how to get dough to rise properly.

An hour later, he completed part of his physical therapy as he paced from the huge wall of windows in the living room, through the kitchen, down a hall, and to the game room door and back. He heard the distinct rhythm of wheeled suitcases rolling across the tile upstairs. Out into the garage. The slam of a door, and then silence.

He was alone in the house. Again.

A heaviness descended upon him, one he'd only hinted at before. He hadn't truly understood why talking to Norah meant so much to him, why having her there hadn't been as hard as he'd originally thought.

With everyone gone again, he realized he hated being

alone, more than he hated Amber for cheating on him, more than he hated wearing his leg brace.

———

"Sterling."

He woke to the sound of an angel's voice. An angel with dark, curly hair. Full lips. Worried eyes.

"Norah." He sat up, glad he'd left on the light in the kitchen but noting the pain in his leg and the darkness beyond the blinds he'd opened. "What time is it?"

"About six." She wrung her hands together as Sterling ran his through his hair. "I came back up to clean, and it started snowing. I don't think I can get back down the mountain tonight."

A chill radiated through the room, causing Sterling to rub his hands along his arms. "Why is it so cold?"

"That's why I woke you up," she said. "I think the furnace went out."

He noticed Norah wore her winter coat, her gloves, and a scarf. He stood, testing his weight on his injured leg though he wore his brace. He'd finally started doing the exercises his doctor wanted, but it only seemed to enflame the pain.

"I tried to relight the pilot on the furnace, but couldn't." Norah looked at him, her eyes asking him for another idea.

"Let's build a fire then." He honestly had no idea where the furnace was located in the cabin and was impressed she did. There were probably two, and he'd have to text his dad to find out where they were.

Satisfied he wouldn't fall, he hobbled over to the wood closet behind the fireplace. "There's matches in the kitchen," he said. "They're in the cupboard above the microwave. Grab 'em, will you?"

Her footsteps scuffled away while he heaved a couple pieces of wood into his arms. "Oh, and there's some lunch bags in the pantry. Grab those too." Thankfully, his mother kept everything stocked even when the house wasn't being used. He'd made enough peanut butter sandwiches for his nieces and nephews to know about the brown bags.

She collected the matches and the paper sacks while he bit back a groan of pain as he knelt to construct a lean-to in the fireplace. He needed a painkiller, fast, but pushed past the stiffness and pain, hoping Norah hadn't noticed.

He crumpled a few bags, stuffing them into the spaces beneath the wood. A few match strikes later, and smoke began to rise from the wood. But it didn't go up the chimney; it started to fill the room.

He mumbled under his breath as Norah coughed and he fumbled to locate the flue. He pulled the lever, and a few minutes later, the smoke had dispersed as the flames built and roared and crackled with heavy amounts of heat.

"There," he said, satisfied that he'd *done something*. "We can stay warm right here."

Norah's panicked gaze flew to his. "We?"

He took a few steps to the windows and looked out at the thick blanket of white obscuring the sky. "It's coming down hard. No way you can drive in that. Unless you have a truck?"

One glance in her direction, and he knew she didn't. Probably a little four-door sedan that weighed less than he did.

"I have some leftover soup upstairs," Norah said, practically running for the stairs.

"Okay." Sterling watched her go, wondering why she was so nervous. A tremor of excitement stirred inside him— maybe a bit of dread at having to choke down that bland soup.

But now that Norah couldn't leave—now that she couldn't retreat to the unheated upper floors—he could learn more about her.

————

Read SNOWED IN WITH THE COWBOY today! A healing cowboy, his maid, and the forbidden relationship that begins when they get snowed in together...

Scan the QR code below to get it!

BOOKS IN THE HORSESHOE HOME RANCH ROMANCE SERIES:

The Redesigned Ranch (Book 1): Jace Lovell, still nursing a wounded heart after being jilted at the altar, has dedicated himself to becoming the best foreman at Horseshoe Home Ranch. When he decides to hire an interior designer to please the ranch owner's wife, he didn't expect to be faced with a familiar face from his past. **Can Belle's patience and faith help Jace find the path to forgiveness and lead them to discover their own slice of happily-ever-after?**

Snowed in with the Cowboy (Book 2): Sterling Maughan, once a renowned snowboarder, is in self-imposed exile at his family cabin after a tragic accident stole his career. Lost and without purpose, solitude is his only companion until an unexpected visitor disrupts his isolation. **Can Norah trust Sterling enough to let him into her life and give their unexpected and forbidden love a chance?**

The Preacher's Daughter (Book 3): Landon Edmunds, a cowboy born and bred, has had his rodeo dreams realized and then dashed by a career-ending injury. Back in his hometown working at Horseshoe Home Ranch, he yearns for a new beginning with a ranch of his own. His sights are set on buying a horse ranch to train rodeo horses, but his plans take a detour when his high school best friend, Megan Palmer, steps back into his life. **Will they choose to follow their hearts, or will they let true love slip through their fingers again?**

Be sure to check out the spinoff series, the Brush Creek Cowboys romances after you read THE PREACHER'S DAUGHTER. Start with BRUSH CREEK COWBOY.

The Cowboy and the Nanny(Book 4): Twelve years ago, Owen Carr traded his roots and his sweetheart in Gold Valley for the bright lights of Nashville, where he found fame as a country music star. But when a tragic accident leaves him single-handedly raising his eight-year-old niece, Marie, he's forced to return home. Overwhelmed and out of his depth, Owen finds a lifeline in a most unexpected place. **As they mend bridges and explore the sparks that still sizzle between them, will they open their hearts to a second chance at love?**

Right Cowboy, Right Time (Book 5): Caleb Chamberlain, a fun-loving cowboy at Horseshoe Home Ranch, has spent the last five years wrestling with the ghosts of his past—a devastating breakup, alcoholism, and a near-fatal accident. Now, he's finally found solace in laughter and the rhythmic simplicity of ranch life. But a chance encounter with a familiar face threatens to upheave his newfound peace. **Can they navigate the shadows of the past to find their happily-ever-after?**

Second Chance Family (Book 6): Ty Barker has been living a carefree existence for the last thirty years. As friends around him found love and started families, Ty filled his time by giving horseback riding lessons and serving on a community service committee. But beneath the jovial surface, he's starting to feel the sting of loneliness. **He knows he wants River Lee in his life—but the question is, can he navigate the delicate steps needed to make her stay with him?**

The Christmas Cowboy Competition (Book 7): Archer Bailey has already had to yield one job to Emersyn "Emery" Enders. So when the opportunity of a cowhand job at Horseshoe Home Ranch presents itself, he keeps it to himself. Emery, whose temporary job is ending but whose responsibilities towards her physically disabled sister aren't, is left in the dark.

As the festive season unfolds, **will Emery and Archer navigate the complexities of the ranch, their close living arrangements, and their personal challenges to discover the love building between them? Or will their rivalry rob them of the greatest Christmas gift of all—true love?**

Love at First Cowboy (Book 8): Elliott Hawthorne, a career cowboy, has just witnessed his best friend and cabinmate forsake bachelorhood for matrimony. He'd be joyous if he weren't so green with envy. When a call about a family accident demands his presence, Elliott finds himself rushing from the ranch to his parents' house to see what's going on with his daddy, where he encounters the most stunning woman he's ever laid eyes on. **But as they encounter the complex dynamics of family responsibilities and personal desires, can their love-at-first-sight grow strong enough withstand the test of time?**

BOOKS IN THE BRUSH CREEK COWBOY ROMANCE SERIES:

Brush Creek Cowboy (Book 1): Former rodeo champion and cowboy Walker Thompson trains horses at Brush Creek Horse Ranch, where he lives a simple life in his cabin with his ten-year-old son. A widower of six years, he's worked with Tess Wagner, a widow who came to Brush Creek to escape the turmoil of her life to give her seven-year-old son a slower pace of life. But Tess's breast cancer is back…

Walker will have to decide if he'd rather spend even a short time with Tess than not have her in his life at all. Tess wants to feel God's love and power, but can she discover and accept God's will in order to find her happy ending?

The Cowboy's Challenge (Book 2): Cowboy and professional roper Justin Jackman has found solitude at Brush Creek Horse Ranch, preferring his time with the animals he trains over dating. With two failed engagements in his past, he's not really interested in getting his heart stomped on again. But when flirty and fun Renee  Martin picks him up at a church ice cream bar--on a bet, no less--he finds himself more than just a little interested. His Gen-X attitudes are attractive to her; her Millennial behaviors drive him nuts. Can Justin look past their differences and take a chance on another engagement?

A Cowboy Proposal (Book 3):
Ted Caldwell has been a retired bronc rider for years, and he thought he was perfectly happy training horses to buck at Brush Creek Ranch. He was wrong. When he meets April Nox, who comes to the ranch to hide her pregnancy from all her friends back in Jackson Hole, Ted realizes he has a huge family-shaped hole in his life. April is embarrassed, heartbroken, and trying to find her extinguished faith. She's never ridden a horse and wants nothing to do with a cowboy ever again. Can Ted and April create a family of happiness and love from a tragedy?

A New Family for the Cowboy (Book 4): Blake Gibbons oversees all the agriculture at Brush Creek Horse Ranch, sometimes moonlighting as a general contractor. When he meets Erin Shields, new in town, at her aunt's bakery, he's instantly smitten. Erin moved to Brush Creek after a divorce that left her penniless, homeless, and a single mother of three children under age eight. She's nowhere near ready to start dating again, but the longer Blake hangs around the bakery, the more she starts to like him. Can Blake and Erin find a way to blend their lifestyles and become a family?

The Cowboy and the Champion (Book 5): Emmett Graves has always had a positive outlook on life. He adores training horses to become barrel racing champions during the day and cuddling with his cat at night. Fresh off her professional rodeo retirement, Molly Brady comes to Brush Creek Horse Ranch as Emmett's protege. He's not thrilled, and she's allergic to cats. Oh, and she'd like to stay cowboy-free, thank you very much. But Emmett's about as cowboy as they come…. Can Emmett and Molly work together without falling in love?

Schooled by the Cowboy (Book 6): Grant Ford spends his days training cattle—when he's not camped out at the elementary school hoping to catch a glimpse of his ex-girlfriend. When principal Shannon Sharpe confronts him and asks him to stay away from the school, the spark between them is instant and hot. Shannon's  expecting a transfer very soon, but she also needs a summer outdoor coordinator—and Grant fits the bill. Just because he's handsome and everything Shannon's ever wanted in a cowboy husband means nothing. Will Grant and Shannon be able to survive the summer or will the Utah heat be too much for them to handle?

Second Chance Ranch: A Three Rivers Ranch Romance™ (Book 1): After his deployment, injured and discharged Major Squire Ackerman returns to Three Rivers Ranch, wanting to forgive Kelly for ignoring him a decade ago. He'd like to provide the stable life she needs, but with old wounds opening and a ranch on the brink of financial collapse, it will take patience and faith to make their second chance possible.

Third Time's the Charm: A Three Rivers Ranch Romance™ (Book 2): First Lieutenant Peter Marshall has a truckload of debt and no way to provide for a family, but Chelsea helps him see past all the obstacles, all the scars. With so many unknowns, can Pete and Chelsea develop the love, acceptance, and faith needed to find their happily ever after?

Fourth and Long: A Three Rivers Ranch Romance™ (Book 3): Commander Brett Murphy goes to Three Rivers Ranch to find some rest and relaxation with his Army buddies. Having his ex-wife show up with a seven-year-old she claims is his son is anything but the R&R he craves. Kate needs to make amends, and Brett needs to find forgiveness, but are they too late to find their happily ever after?

Fifth Generation Cowboy: A Three Rivers Ranch Romance™ (Book 4): Tom Lovell has watched his friends find their true happiness on Three Rivers Ranch, but every-where he looks, he only sees friends. Rose Reyes has been bringing her daughter out to the ranch for equine therapy for months, but it doesn't seem to be working. Her challenges with Mari are just as frustrating as ever. Could Tom be exactly what Rose needs? Can he remove his friendship blinders and find love with someone who's been right in front of him all this time?

Sixth Street Love Affair: A Three Rivers Ranch Romance™ (Book 5): After losing his wife a few years back, Garth Ahlstrom thinks he's ready for a second chance at love. But Juliette Thompson has a secret that could destroy their budding relationship. Can they find the strength, patience, and faith to make things work?

The Seventh Sergeant: A Three Rivers Ranch Romance™ (Book 6): Life has finally started to settle down for Sergeant Reese Sanders after his devastating injury overseas. Discharged from the Army and now with a good job at Courage Reins, he's finally found happiness—until a horrific fall puts him right back where he was years ago: Injured and depressed. Carly Watters, Reese's new veteran care coordinator, dislikes small towns almost as much as she loathes cowboys. But she finds herself faced with both when she gets assigned to Reese's case. Do they have the humility and faith to make their relationship more than professional?

Eight Second Ride: A Three Rivers Ranch Romance™ (Book 7): Ethan Greene loves his work at Three Rivers Ranch, but he can't seem to find the right woman to settle down with. When sassy yet vulnerable Brynn Bowman shows up at the ranch to recruit him back to the rodeo circuit, he takes a different approach with the barrel racing champion. His patience and newfound faith pay off when a friendship--and more--starts with Brynn. But she wants out of the rodeo circuit right when Ethan wants to rejoin. Can they find the path God wants them to take and still stay together?

The Ninth Inning: A Three Rivers Ranch Romance™ (Book 8): The Christmas season has never felt like such a burden to boutique owner Andrea Larsen. But with Mama gone and the holidays upon her, Andy finds herself wishing she hadn't been so quick to judge her former boyfriend, cowboy Lawrence Collins. Well, Lawrence hasn't forgotten about Andy either, and he devises a plan to get her out to the ranch so they can reconnect. Do they have the faith and humility to patch things up and start a new relationship?

Ten Days in Town: A Three Rivers Ranch Romance™ (Book 9): Sandy Keller is tired of the dating scene in Three Rivers. Though she owns the pancake house, she's looking for a fresh start, which means an escape from the town where she grew up. When her older brother's best friend, Tad Jorgensen, comes to town for the holidays, it is a balm to his weary soul. A helicopter tour guide who experienced a near-death experience, he's looking to start over too--but in Three Rivers. Can Sandy and Tad navigate their troubles to find the path God wants them to take--and discover true love--in only ten days?

Eleven Year Reunion: A Three Rivers Ranch Romance™ (Book 10): Pastry chef extraordinaire, Grace Lewis has moved to Three Rivers to help Heidi Ackerman open a bakery in Three Rivers. Grace relishes the idea of starting over in a town where no one knows about her failed cupcakery. She doesn't expect to run into her old high school boyfriend, Jonathan Carver. A carpenter working at Three Rivers Ranch, Jon's in town against his will. But with Grace now on the scene, Jon's thinking life in Three Rivers is suddenly looking up. But with her focus on baking and his disdain for small towns, can they make their eleven year reunion stick?

The Twelfth Town: A Three Rivers Ranch Romance™ (Book 11): Newscaster Taryn Tucker has had enough of life on-screen. She's bounced from town to town before arriving in Three Rivers, completely alone and completely anonymous-- just the way she now likes it. She takes a job cleaning at Three Rivers Ranch, hoping for a chance to figure out who she is and where God wants her. When she meets happy-go-lucky cowhand Kenny Stockton, she doesn't expect sparks to fly. Kenny's always been "the best friend" for his female friends, but the pull between him and Taryn can't be denied. Will they have the courage and faith necessary to make their opposite worlds mesh?

Lucky Number Thirteen: A Three Rivers Ranch Romance™ (Book 12): Tanner Wolf, a rodeo champion ten times over, is excited to be riding in Three Rivers for the first time since he left his philandering ways and found religion. Seeing his old friends Ethan and Brynn is therapuetic--until a terrible accident lands him in the hospital. With his rodeo career over, Tanner thinks maybe he'll stay in town--and it's not just because his nurse, Summer Hamblin, is the prettiest woman he's ever met. But Summer's the queen of first dates, and as she looks for a way to make a relationship with the transient rodeo star work Summer's not sure she has the fortitude to go on a second date. Can they find love among the tragedy?

The Curse of February Four-teenth: A Three Rivers Ranch Romance™ (Book 13): Cal Hodgkins, cowboy veterinarian at Bowman's Breeds, isn't planning to meet anyone at the masked dance in small-town Three Rivers. He just wants to get his bachelor friends off his back and sit on the sidelines to drink his punch. But when he sees a woman dressed in gorgeous butterfly wings and cowgirl boots with blue stitching, he's smitten. Too bad she runs away from the dance before he can get her name, leaving only her boot behind...

Fifteen Minutes of Fame: A Three Rivers Ranch Romance™ (Book 14): Navy Richards is thirty-five years of tired—tired of dating the same men, working a demanding job, and getting her heart broken over and over again. Her aunt has always spoken highly of the matchmaker in Three Rivers, Texas, so she takes a six-month sabbatical from her high-stress job as a pediatric nurse, hops on a bus, and meets with the matchmaker. Then she meets Gavin Redd. He's handsome, he's hardworking, and he's a cowboy. But is he an Aquarius too? Navy's not making a move until she knows for sure...

Sixteen Steps to Fall in Love: A Three Rivers Ranch Romance™ (Book 15): A chance encounter at a dog park sheds new light on the tall, talented Boone that Nicole can't ignore. As they get to know each other better and start to dig into each other's past, Nicole is the one who wants to run. This time from her growing admiration and attachment to Boone. From her aging parents. From herself.

But Boone feels the attraction between them too, and he decides he's tired of running and ready to make Three Rivers his permanent home. **Can Boone and Nicole use their faith to overcome their differences and find a happily-ever-after together?**

The Sleigh on Seventeenth Street: A Three Rivers Ranch Romance™ (Book 16): A cowboy with skills as an electrician tries a relationship with a down-on-her luck plumber. Can Dylan and Camila make water and electricity play nicely together this Christmas season? Or will they get shocked as they try to make their relationship work?

The First Lady of Three Rivers Ranch: A Three Rivers Ranch Romance™ (Book 17): Heidi Duffin has been dreaming about opening her own bakery since she was thirteen years old. She scrimped and saved for years to afford baking and pastry school in San Francisco. And now she only has one year left before she's a certified pastry chef. Frank Ackerman's father has recently retired, and he's taken over the largest cattle ranch in the Texas Panhandle. A horseman through and through, he's also nearing thirty-one and looking for someone to bring love and joy to a homestead that's been dominated by men for a decade. But when he convinces Heidi to come clean the cowboy cabins, she changes all that. But the siren's call of a bakery is still loud in Heidi's ears, even if she's also seeing a future with Frank. Can she rely on her faith in ways she's never had to before or will their relationship end when summer does?

Eighteen Bowties and Counting: A Three Rivers Ranch Romance™ (Book 18): He's her older brother's best friend and completely off-limits. She's got a way with horses...and a heart condition. Can Beau and Charlotte navigate close quarters to find their happily-ever-after?

ABOUT LIZ

Liz Isaacson writes inspirational romance, usually set in Texas, or Wyoming, or anywhere else horses and cowboys exist. She lives in Utah, where she writes full-time, takes her two dogs to the park everyday, and eats a lot of veggies while writing. Find her on her website at feelgoodfiction-books.com